PRAISE FOR

THE DEVIL YOU KNOW

A VOYA Perfect Ten

"A sexy and suspenseful read that kept me thinking of the characters long after I finished the book."
—Katie McGarry, author of the Pushing the Limits series and *Nowhere but Here*

"This suspenseful contemporary tale delivers the believable adventure story of an eighteen-year-old who embarks on a rebellious quest and finds romance and danger."
—*VOYA*

"The spark between Noah and Cadie is delicious, and the slow build of darkness throughout the story is the kind of terrifying that teens will enjoy....A must-buy."
—*SLJ*

"A suspenseful romantic thriller."
—*Kirkus Reviews*

"As the stakes increase and the opportunities for escape deep in the Everglades narrow, the Hitchcockian conclusion is swift and satisfying."
—*Booklist*

Books by Trish Doller

Something Like Normal
Where the Stars Still Shine
The Devil You Know

THE DEVIL YOU KNOW

TRISH DOLLER

BLOOMSBURY

NEW YORK   LONDON   OXFORD   NEW DELHI   SYDNEY

First published in the United States of America in June 2015
by Bloomsbury Children's Books
Paperback edition published in June 2016
www.bloomsbury.com

Bloomsbury is a registered trademark of Bloomsbury Publishing Plc

For information about permission to reproduce selections from this book, write to
Permissions, Bloomsbury Children's Books, 1385 Broadway, New York, New York 10018
Bloomsbury books may be purchased for business or promotional use. For information on bulk
purchases please contact Macmillan Corporate and Premium Sales Department at
specialmarkets@macmillan.com

The Library of Congress has cataloged the hardcover edition as follows:
Doller, Trish.
The devil you know / by Trish Doller.
pages   cm
Summary: Exhausted and rebellious after three years of working for her father
and mothering her brother, eighteen-year-old Arcadia "Cadie" Wells joins
two cousins who are camping their way through Florida.
ISBN 978-1-61963-416-9 (hardcover) • ISBN 978-1-61963-417-6 (e-book)
[1. Psychopaths—Fiction. 2. Murder—Fiction. 3. Camping—Fiction. 4. Fathers and daughters—
Fiction. 5. Single-parent families—Fiction. 6. Florida—Fiction.] I. Title.
PZ7.D7055Dev 2015   [Fic]—dc23   2014023032

ISBN 978-1-68119-022-8 (paperback)

Book design by Amanda Bartlett
Typeset by Westchester Book Composition
Printed and bound in the U.S.A. by Berryville Graphics Inc., Berryville, Virginia
2 4 6 8 10 9 7 5 3 1

To all the girls who know what they want.
And to all the girls who don't.

Hell is empty, and all the devils are here.
—William Shakespeare, *The Tempest*

CHAPTER 1

CHAPTER 1

Freedom is ticking its way around the face of the old clock above the door—*so close, so close, so close*—when Justin comes into the market and I die a tiny, unnoticeable death. Not so much because he's here in my dad's grocery store with his arm draped around the girl from Alachua who took my place on the soccer team, but because they're stopping in for a twelve-pack on their way out to O'Leno. Summer Fridays were our thing and it never occurred to me that Fridays would ever be anything other than ours. That I could be replaced so thoroughly.

I don't miss him. Not at all. But I miss having someone to lie with on the big moss-covered log beside the river just talking about nothing. Or not talking. I miss the feel of his warm hands on my bare skin under the tree-speckled sunshine. I miss his mouth on mine until our lips are swollen and raw. His dark-blue eyes meet mine over the top of his new girlfriend's head, and I'm lying. I miss all of that so much it hurts.

Until now the plan was to get a head start with my Saturday off—a rare and precious commodity—watching *Finding Nemo* with my little brother until his bedtime, then stay up until the wee hours of the morning planning trips to places I've never been. Thumbing through yard sale guidebooks—some from countries that aren't even countries anymore—and pinning my someday destinations on the maps that cover the bruise-purple paint on my bedroom walls. Maybe Machu Picchu. Or Iceland to see the northern lights. Or diving in Fiji, even though I don't dive. Yet. Until now I was looking forward to putting on my pajamas and imagining a life beyond High Springs, Florida. Now the prospect of sitting home alone just . . . sucks.

Before I have time to dwell, Justin's stupid twin brother, Jason, blasts through the door, making the bells on the handle rattle as if they've been caught in a blender. He's built like an oversize LEGO man and looks so different from Justin that it's hard to imagine them related, let alone sharing the same womb.

"Hey there, Sparkles." Jason doesn't hoist so much as launch himself onto the counter beside me. He's wearing a T-shirt with ripped-off sleeves so I can see the pimples on his shoulder and deodorant bits sticking to his armpit hair. "A bunch of us are hanging out tonight down at the river. Wanna come skinny-dipping with me?"

Eleven years ago I was cast in the role of Sparkles the Snowflake in the elementary school Christmas play, so Jason started calling me Sparkles. Not that Arcadia Wells is much better, but I like my name because according to the beat-up old baby name book with yellowed pages that my mom used to name me, Arcadia means "adventurous." I like to think that was her dream for me, too. That one day I really will escape this place. Even though everyone else calls me Cadie, Jason still thinks the nickname Sparkles is as funny as it was when we were seven. Of course, I'm of the opinion that Jason Kendrick is likely to marry his own sister, so I try not to let him get to me.

"Not if we were the last two people on earth," I say, watching Justin slide his hands up and down the arms of the girl from Alachua, keeping her warm in the chilly beer aisle the way he always did for me. Jason donkey-laughs as if I'm joking and I feel snot trickle from my nose.

I will not cry.

I refuse to cry.

Instead, I shove Jason off the counter.

"Come on, Sparkles, don't be like that." He pouts. "It'll be fun, and maybe I'll even let you—" He pumps his fist in front of his mouth and pushes his tongue against the inside of his cheek. My face catches fire, and I feel like I'm going to be sick. What Justin and I did alone together was private. Something I've never done with anyone else. Ever. Would he really tell Jason?

Anger bounces through me like a pinball, pinging off my insides until I'm lit up with it. Justin brings a twelve-pack to the cash register as if it's still our Friday. As if any of this is okay. In my head I tell him to go buy his beer somewhere else from now on. In my head I tell him to go to hell. But in the real world, I ring up the beer without telling him anything at all, and he gives me money enough to pay for it.

On the walk home I decide I'm going up to the state park tonight even if it means having to watch Justin making out with his new girlfriend. She's not all that new. He started dating her last year, about three weeks after he dumped me. Just before Coach Wainwright gave her my spot on the team. I can't hate the girl from Alachua because it's not her fault I had to quit. Dad was barely holding it together after Mom died, so someone had to look after Danny and run the household. Not sure I'm doing a very good job of it, especially when the house comes into view. The paint is flaking off the shutters and our lawn is more weeds than grass, and I'm embarrassed by how shabby it's become.

Dad is parked at the kitchen table with his ledger book

and a beer. Even though I've tried to persuade him to use the computer to keep his books, he says there's a kind of Zen in doing it on paper. I drop a kiss on the top of his head, noticing a few extra strands of gray amid the brown, as my little brother comes running in from the living room and hugs me around my butt. He'll be four soon and sometimes he thinks he's too big a boy for hugs, but apparently today is not one of those days.

"Hello there, Mister Boone." I ruffle his pale blond hair. Towheaded is what Mom always called us, although a couple of nights ago, in a fit of late-night boredom, I dyed mine a streaky ginger-gold and chopped it just below my chin, a move I can't decide was stupid or genius. It's a fine line, really.

Anyway, ever since I read my brother a storybook about Daniel Boone, Danny insists that's his name, too. I asked the guidance counselor at school if it was weird, especially since nothing in our house has been normal for a long time, but she assured me he would grow out of it. I guess Danny's harboring the fantasy that he's an eighteenth-century frontiersman is no crazier than my believing I'll ever actually scale the citadel at Machu Picchu.

"How about some ravioli tonight?" I tie on the owl-print apron Mom and I made together when she first taught me how to sew. She wore it whenever she cooked, even if she was doing something as simple as tearing open a packet of macaroni and cheese-powder. Mom was special that way and, well . . . it sounds a little silly, but whenever I wear the apron I feel as if her arms are around me. Holding me together.

"Raviolis!" Danny throws his arms in the air, doing a one-man wave. I should be relieved, but his current level of enthusiasm is no guarantee he'll eat it. I can make the same sauce three times, and the fourth time he'll declare it yucky. "Can I help?"

He tears the iceberg lettuce into tiny pieces—too small for salad, but I let him do it his own way—while I heat up a jar of spaghetti sauce and drop frozen ravioli into a boiling pot. Danny chatters to me about the adventures his Wonder Woman doll was having before I got home from work. She used to belong to me, but I gave him the doll when he was old enough not to chew on her legs. Despite the conversations we've had about how all toys are for all kids, he's starting to gravitate toward traditionally "boy" stuff like dump trucks, pirates, and anything that requires explosive sound effects. Still, he loves the hell out of Wonder Woman. Dad rolls his eyes at our conversation, but he never discourages Danny because he knows Mom would feel the same way as I do.

Before long, dinner is on the table, and after Dad says grace, he asks me if everything went okay at the store today. Aside from Justin and his illegal beer purchase (which Dad doesn't need to know about), we didn't have very many customers. I'm reluctant to spoil dinner with the bad news. "It was fine. A little quiet. Maybe Rhea will have a beer rush before closing."

Dad's sigh is a black hole that crushes all the happiness in the room. I know it weighs heavy that the store loses a little more every year, and I feel like it's somehow my fault, even though I know better. We can't compete with the Winn-Dixie. And Mom was the heartbeat that kept everything alive. The store. The house. Us.

I blink away tears and focus on my ravioli. The phone rings, and Dad's chair scrapes across the tile as he gets up to answer. "Hello . . . oh, hey, Ed . . ."

Uncle Eddie is always calling with fictional home improvement projects he can't complete without my father, a man who couldn't hammer his way out of a wet paper bag. Dad thinks I don't know that they just sit in the garage, watching documentaries and drinking beer, but I do. When it was a once-a-month thing it wasn't a problem, but now he's over there a couple times a week. Add late nights at the grocery store, town council meetings, and historical preservation committee, and me and Daniel Boone are practically orphans.

Avoidance. Dad's coping mechanism of choice.

"Can we watch *Nemo*?" Danny, looking upside down at me while I clear away his plate, is probably as tempting as it gets, but there's no way I'm staying home tonight.

"Listen, buddy—"

"Cadie." Dad rests the receiver back in the cradle. I'm pretty sure we're the last family on the planet with a landline. The only people who ever call us on it are solicitors and Uncle Eddie. Even Grandma Ruth calls our cell phones, and she's pushing eighty. "I know tonight is supposed to be your night off—"

"Tonight is my night off. *Is*." I put added emphasis to the word, but he doesn't notice.

"But Eddie needs—"

"Have you looked at our house lately?" I ask. "Maybe Uncle Eddie could help you for a change."

"Arcadia June." Anger bubbles under the surface of Dad's voice, like water just before boiling point. "Being a single parent is not easy, and I would appreciate it if—"

"Oh, I know how not easy it is," I interrupt, going down the hall to my bedroom. Dad follows. "I mean, who mows the lawn? Me. Who cleans the house? Me. Who does the laundry? Oh! That's right. Me again. I take Danny to the doctor when he's sick, tuck him in every night, and chase away the black-and-yellow bee monster under his bed. And, until last weekend, I did all that while going to high school. Tonight is my night off. Deal with it."

"Cadie." He's spoiling for a fight, but I refuse to engage. I nudge my bedroom door with my foot, and as it swings dangerously close to his nose I tell him I'm going to

O'Leno with some friends. "I don't know exactly what time I'll be home," I say. "Maybe tonight. Maybe tomorrow morning. Maybe I won't be back until Sunday."

I realize my attitude kind of sucks, and God knows my dad works as hard as I do, but it feels like I'm always the one making concessions. Back when I was a freshman and Danny was a baby, he got his days and nights mixed up. It was me who cut a path in the carpet trying to get him to sleep, and I missed so much school we got a warning letter from the district. I get that we need Dad's income from the store, but sometimes I think he forgets Danny is his child. And that I am his child, too.

My white undershirt and shorts end up in a heap on the floor as I rummage through my closet. I have this whole second wardrobe I've collected but never really worn because I'm saving it for someday. I don't know. Maybe tonight is when someday begins.

I choose a vintage navy-blue polka-dot dress I picked up at a consignment shop in Gainesville and the brown motorcycle boots that set me back an entire grocery store paycheck. I could use a shower and I'm not completely sure my day-two bangs will pass for shiny, but Dad is still on the other side of the door, lecturing me about responsibility and family sacrifice. I've given up soccer. I've given up Justin. I'm not sure what's left to sacrifice, but it definitely won't be my night off.

My bangs get braided away from my face before I pause in front of the mirror to check out the new me. Then I roll my eyes at myself because I'm just the old me in a dress. I've never worn one for a campfire party before, and all this exposed skin will be a feast for mosquitoes and deer ticks, but I look good. Maybe even a little better than good.

I shove Justin's denim jacket—one he won't ever be getting back—into my inherited-from-Mom leather knapsack, along with my wallet, keys, and a bottle of bug lotion, and then call Duane Imler.

"You wouldn't happen to be going past O'Leno, would you?" I ask when he answers. "I could use a lift."

Duane graduated a year ago and drives a flatbed tow truck for a local company. He was my second boyfriend for about three weeks when I was in eighth grade and he was a newly minted freshman. Even though we never went anywhere because he couldn't drive—he'd ride his bike over to my house to hang out—I thought I was so cool "dating" a boy in high school. My first kiss was with Duane. I've never told him that it was like having a plunger stuck to my face, but clearly he must have refined his technique, since Jessica Shiver is marrying him this coming Christmas.

Anyway, our friendship survived the breakup and I still have the butterfly necklace that turned my neck green that Duane gave me for my fourteenth birthday.

He's one of those guys who's okay with spending the rest of his life in High Springs, and I'm not looking down my nose when I say that because some of us are meant to stay. He's happy. Maybe more than I can say about myself.

"Where are you?" he asks.

"About to climb out my bedroom window."

He laughs. "I'll be right over."

I wait until the tow truck comes around the corner, then slide up the screen and lower myself the short distance to the ground. I run through the too-tall grass and climb into the cab as Dad comes out the front door, wearing his Zeus-about-to-throw-lightning-bolts face. Our walls are like paper. There was no way this was ever going to be a clean getaway.

"I'll see you tomorrow," I call out, waving at him through the open passenger window as Duane accelerates away from the house. "And don't forget that Daniel Boone won't eat his eggs if they're even a little bit runny."

CHAPTER 2

CHAPTER 2

From the driver's seat, Duane whistles, low and wolf-ish, eyeing my dress. It's got a scoop neck edged with a little plaid ruffle. "Damn, Cadie. You're going to break some hearts up there at the campground tonight."

"Really? You think?" I'm secretly thrilled at the idea of being capable of breaking someone's heart. Maybe that's the new Arcadia Wells. Beautiful. Dangerous. Duane brings me back to reality with a well-placed flick to my temple.

"Don't let it go to your head," he says. "And don't go thinking you're going to win Justin back, either, because that ain't happening."

"I wasn't thinking that."

"Liar," he says, as his walkie-talkie-type phone chirps

and the dispatcher from the towing company tells him about a blown tire out on I-75. Duane acknowledges the job, then looks at me. "He's headed for Gainesville in the fall, and you'll bust outta this town the first chance you get, so there's no point to messing with his feelings."

"He broke up with me, remember?"

"And you know why, Cadie, so don't play stupid."

Between work, school, and raising a little brother, I didn't have time enough for my boyfriend. Truth be told, I still don't, not even with school no longer a part of the equation. I've stepped into my mom's shoes while my own grow dusty in the back of my closet.

"Besides," Duane continues, "he's happy with Gabrielle."

That's her name, the girl from Alachua, but I like to pretend I don't know it. Immature, I know, but it's impossible to be graceful *all* the time over being dumped. Sometimes I'm a jerk.

"I don't want him back anyway." It's a lie. Half lie. I don't even know anymore. Seeing Justin at the store today has me all twisted up, but honestly, most days I really don't think about him all that much.

Duane still looks skeptical. "Good."

Even though it's already a fifteen-minute drive from my house to the park entrance, he pays the five bucks so I don't have to walk all the way to the campsite, which is a really sweet thing to do. Parked beside the ranger station is a black convertible muscle car that swivels Duane's neck. "Damn. That's a '69 Cougar."

"It's pretty."

"Sweetheart, that car's more than pretty," he says. "And that one right there's gotta be worth about twenty-five grand. Probably still has the original 351."

"Now you're just talking gibberish," I say. "What I'm wondering is why someone would use a testosterone machine like that to haul canoes."

Hitched to the back bumper, below a Georgia license plate, is a trailer loaded with a pair of red boats, and standing beside the driver's door is a guy who looks like he stepped right off page eleven of the L.L. Bean catalog. Dark-brown outdoorsy hair, red plaid shirt with rolled-up sleeves, expensive hiking boots, excellent calf muscles. I stop thinking about how he doesn't match the car when he aims a boy-next-door smile in my direction and my insides shimmer like a New Year's Eve sparkler.

"Hey! There's a party on the Magnolia campground loop." I shout it out the window at him. "You should come."

The guy gives me a thumbs-up, which could mean he's coming or he's humoring the crazy girl in the tow truck. Either way, I asked him to the party. That's what the all-new Arcadia Wells would do. Although she might have been a little more sophisticated about it.

Duane laughs. "Subtle."

"Shut up." I turn away from the window, embarrassment creeping warm up my neck, and punch him on the shoulder. The guy at the ranger station probably isn't into girls who bum rides from tow truck drivers, but I sure do like his smile.

"Here's fine to drop me," I say when we reach the Magnolia loop. The Jake brakes *whoosh* as Duane stops the truck and I lean over to kiss his scruffy cheek. "You're the best. Thanks."

"Anytime," he says. "You know that."

"You think you'll come by later to hang out?"

"Nah." He shakes his head. "Soon as I answer the call on I-75, I'm going home for dinner and a movie with Jess. Besides, you'll probably be making out with '69 Cougar before too long. But if you need a ride home, or anything at all, you let me know, okay?"

"Yes, sir." I give him a little salute. "Love you."

He tells me to shut up—which has always been his way of letting me know he loves me, too—and then his truck rumbles away.

I follow the dirt-and-gravel road, my boots making a satisfying and badass gunslinger-at-high-noon kind of sound as I pass RVs, campers, and tents—most of them from out of state—until I reach the campsite. The fire and the party are already crackling, with people sprawled out on blankets and sitting on lawn chairs in a ring around the fire pit. I recognize almost everyone, except for a dreadlocked hippie couple who may or may not be smoking pot.

A few people call out to me as I make my way beneath the cypress trees to the galvanized feed trough full of ice and beer. At the sound of my name, Justin looks up from the grill where he's cooking hot dogs and burgers.

"Hey, uh—hey, Cadie," he stammers.

I nod in his direction and throw him my sweetest smile. "Justin."

A couple of steps more and I turn to see if he's watching my ass. He is. Happy, my foot. But as I thrust my arm deep into the ice to find the coldest beer, I think Duane is right. Maybe I could get Justin back tonight (or maybe my dress-wearing, inviting-cute-boys-to-parties ego is a little out of control), but I need to leave him alone. I don't want backward drama. I want forward adventure.

I'm popping open my can when Jason crashes out of the woods, zipping up his fly. When he sees me, he gets a big dumb smile on his face. "Arcadia Wells, gracing us with her presence at our little soiree."

"Sometimes it's good to walk among the peasants," I say, then take a sip of beer. Being the coldest in the trough still doesn't make it taste very good. "And listen to you, talking all fancy. Seems like just yesterday you were sounding out the words while reading. Oh, wait. That *was* yesterday."

He laughs and hugs me, smashing my face against his shirt, which smells of campfire and weed and boy stink. "It's okay to admit, Sparkles, that all those insults are just your way of hiding the fact that you really want to bounce up and down on my johnson."

"Your johnson? God, you're classy."

"I know, right? Going skinny-dipping with me later?"

"If you're lucky and I'm desperate."

He presses sloppy beer lips against my cheek and releases me. "Desperation is my favorite quality in a woman."

"I know this," I call over my shoulder as I walk toward the fire pit, where I've spotted a group of my former teammates sitting on a blanket. "I've met your ex-girlfriends."

"Cadie! Oh my God, I love your hair!" Hallie Kernaghan waves me over and pats the empty spot between her and Carmen Ruiz. I sit. "It's been too long since you've hung out with us. Where have you been? How are you?" Hallie peppers words at me as she rests her head on my shoulder, something she always used to do on bus rides home from games. "We miss you on the team."

Other voices chime in agreement, but I can't help wondering if they miss the girl or the goalkeeper, because the extent of our interactions at school this past year have been reduced to quick hellos in the school hallways. Nobody tells you that's how it works when you're no longer on the team, but that's how it works. We're still friendly, but we're not quite friends anymore. Letting go was easier than I thought, and maybe I just miss being their goalkeeper. I'm not sure. "I miss you guys, too."

Most of the other girls are younger than me so I don't know them very well. And when they start talking about how excited they are about their upcoming training camp at the University of Florida, I sit and half listen for a while so as not to be impolite. It hurts to think about the soccer camps I've missed. The games. The anticipation that would coil in the pit of my stomach when the action started coming down the field toward me. The conversation gets kind of painful, so I excuse myself for another beer, even though the one I have is practically full.

I'm standing at the trough with two beers I am not interested in drinking when the guy with the '69 Cougar walks up to the party. He glances around, and my stomach goes jumping-bean nervous. Should I approach him? Wait for him to spot me? Then I get a little panicked that maybe he's not looking for me at all. Maybe he's already noticed Hallie with her pretty blue eyes. Or Carmen's dark, sexy curls. Or Lindsey Buck, who is the girl most likely to be discovered at a shopping mall by a modeling agency. I've just about talked myself out of him when his eyes meet mine across the fire. He gives me the same adorable smile as before and skirts the pit to reach me.

"You came." Handing him my spare beer is oddly intimate considering I don't even know him, but it's only going to waste and he accepts it without a second thought. "I wasn't sure you would, given, you know, the weirdness of the invitation."

"I've never been hollered at from a tow truck before." The can hisses as he cracks it open. "How could I resist?"

I laugh. "I'm Cadie."

He wipes his palm on the side of his shorts before shaking my hand. "Nice to meet you, Cadie. I'm Matt."

Matt.

I like his name. I like the bony bump of his wrist below his brown leather watchband. I like the barely-there sun freckles trailing across the bridge of his nose. His dark hair curls out every which way from the bottom edge of his Red Sox ball cap. If he took it off, there'd probably be an indentation in his hair, and I'm pretty sure I'd like that, too. But the sum of the parts is almost too much for me to handle. He's so well made, and I'm standing here feeling like half-off day at the thrift store, and my brain just dries up.

"Are you from around here?" Matt asks, and I notice the subtle drop of the *r* sound from the word "here" that marks him as a New Englander. Maybe Boston with that ball cap.

"Sadly, yes," I say. "Just a small town girl . . ."

Matt catches my reference to the old Journey anthem and offers up his fist for me to bump. "Don't stop believing, Cadie," he says as our knuckles touch.

"So you're wearing a Boston hat, but your car has Georgia plates," I say, as we claim a pair of upended milk crates on the upwind side of the fire pit. I watch Matt's face, wondering if he thinks we're the biggest group of rednecks he's ever encountered, but he stretches his hiking boots toward the fire like he doesn't notice. Like he's one of us. Except most of the girls at the party are looking at him as if they're thankful he's not. "What's your story?"

"I'm actually from Maine," Matt says. "But the car belonged to my grandmother who recently died. She lived in Savannah."

"I'm sorry."

"Thanks." There's a hint of sadness in his half smile that makes me want to give him a hug, but I keep my hands to myself. "My family came down for the funeral, and afterward my cousin and I decided to road-trip south, camping and paddling our way through Florida. One last adventure before he shackles himself to the workforce for the next fifty years."

"Sounds like fun."

"So far it's been great," Matt says. "Speaking of fun . . . anything around here we shouldn't miss?"

"Since you've got your own canoes, you can pretty much launch anywhere," I say. "You could paddle from here down to River Sink, or you could launch from the outpost out on 441 and go downstream to one of the springs. Lily Spring is always interesting because of Naked Ed."

"Naked Ed?"

"He's basically a nudist who takes care of the spring," I explain. "He keeps a little thatched hut and wears a loin-cloth when people are around."

"Yes! That's exactly what I'm talking about." Matt's smile is like the sun, and it warms me all over. "Have you seen him?"

"I haven't."

He nudges me gently with his elbow. "Maybe you should come with us."

Maybe this is my chance for a little forward adventure. A small rebellion with a side of cute boy. I smile back. "Maybe I should."

"So would it be fair to assume you don't have a boyfriend?"

My eyes go to Justin and Gabrielle—a stupid habit I can't seem to break—who are snuggled like birds on the tailgate of his silver pickup. They seem to be incapable of keeping their hands off each other. It was never like that with Justin and me, and I have no idea why. Maybe because my hands were always full.

"If I did, I probably wouldn't be sitting here with you right now." My dormant flirting skills seem to be warming up. "So that would be a very fair assumption. Of course, I might have a girlfriend."

He laughs. Not in a mean way—like it's incomprehensible that I could be attracted to girls—but as if I've outsmarted him. "Do you?" he asks.

"No girlfriends."

"That works out well because I don't have any girlfriends, either."

I can't envision a world in which a guy as good-looking as Matt is single, but since he won't be in High Springs for more than a couple of days, I choose to buy what he's selling. "Perfect."

He pulls his feet away from the fire and stands. "I'm going to grab another beer. Want one?"

"I'm good." I hold up my original, mostly full can. "But thanks."

I sit by myself for a minute or two, wondering if Matt expects me to wait for him or if he's moving on to someone else. Especially when Lindsey Buck approaches him at the beer trough and he gives her the same only-girl-in-the-room smile he gave me. I wilt a little, embarrassed that I thought he meant it only for me. Embarrassed that I've lost touch with my friends to the point where my closest relationship is with Jason Kendrick. Embarrassed that even in a crowd of people—many of whom I've known since kindergarten—I'm alone.

I should go home.

Duane would come fetch me, but I haven't been here very long and I don't want to ask him to drive back already. To save some face and buy some time, I decide to take a walk down by the river.

"Hey, are you leaving?" Matt returns with a fresh beer—and Lindsey—as I'm hoisting my knapsack onto my shoulder.

"I, um . . . just need to go to the bathroom."

"I'll walk you there," he offers, but when Lindsey's smile droops, it's definitely time to go. I have no claim on Matt, and I'm starting to rethink the appeal of pajama pants and talking cartoon fish.

"That's really sweet," I say. "But it's okay. I'll be back."

CHAPTER 3

I'm headed away from the party, frogs and crickets serenading me like I'm some sort of backwoods Disney princess, when I spot the '69 Cougar parked just a handful of campsites away. The canoe trailer is unhitched from the car, and there's a guy—Matt's cousin, I presume, unless they're getting robbed—bent over the open trunk. His T-shirt rides up, exposing a slash of bare skin and a pair of back dimples that sit just above the droop of his faded jeans. I slow my pace because it's the kind of back that deserves to be admired for a good long while. And because, apparently, my hormones are working overtime. Then he turns around with a big red cooler in his hands, and I'm so busted.

His maple syrup eyes and nearly black hair are close

enough to Matt's that it's clear they fell from the same family tree, but this guy is a broken-in version. Older. And now that I can see the whole of him, he's made up of so many interesting parts I'm not sure what to look at first.

Maybe the Frankenstein scar, white and jagged against his tanned skin, that starts in his hairline and travels down his forehead, slicing his dark eyebrow in half. It's angry. Violent. Probably not the kind of scar that comes with a cute story about how he fell learning to ride his first two-wheeler or got hit with a baseball in Little League.

Or the colorful constellation of old-school nautical tattoos—sailing ships, anchors and ropes, bell-helmeted divers, and naked mermaids, connected by hundreds upon hundreds of tiny stars—that begin beneath the sleeves of his T-shirt and wind their way to his wrists.

My eyes travel back up to his nose, which sits off-kilter at the bridge as if it's been broken. To his hair cropped to peach fuzz. To the corner of his mouth that lifts in a grin that acknowledges that I'm checking him out—and God, do I want to know him.

He places the cooler on the ground, and his boots scuff up the dust as he catches up with me. "Hey, um—hi."

"Hi." He's so tall. The top of my head would fit perfectly beneath his chin, and that thought requires a deep breath before I speak again. "I'm Cadie."

"Noah." His big fingers tap the crackled Trojan All-Stars logo imprinted in the middle of his T-shirt. I want to know what this logo means. The significance of the string of wooden beads around his wrist. Where he comes from. What his mouth tastes like. I say hi again, then feel my face get hot with stupidity because we've already said hello. Because looking at him is like trying to stare at the sun and not caring that you might go blind. And because he's looking at me, too.

"Where you headed?" he asks, falling into step beside me.

"Just taking a walk," I say. He doesn't have the same accent as Matt, but I don't tell him that because it might seem weird and stalker-y. Especially since he isn't aware that I know who he is. Not sure how to tell him that, either, so I don't. "Where you from?"

"Oakland by way of Maine by way of Savannah. Do you mind if I walk with you?"

"Sounds complicated," I say, and I like that we're carrying on two conversations at once. I like that his honey-and-gravel voice seems to come from somewhere deep and secret and special. "And no, I don't mind a bit."

"The short version," he says, "is my cousin Matt and I are camping our way down the state toward Flamingo. Ever hear of it?"

I shake my head.

"It's a deserted town at the end of mainland Florida and surrounded by Everglades. Pretty remote," Noah says.

"Whatever gets you excited."

"Not a fan of camping?"

"Oh, no. I love camping," I say, watching a grin kick up at the corner of his mouth, and it's like this invisible thread stretches between us, connecting us. Something in common. Even if it's just an affinity for sleeping on the ground. "But given the choice of Florida or not Florida, I'd always pick not Florida."

"Where would you go?"

"Maybe Oakland by way of Savannah and Maine."

My brazen-girl flirting works like magic, turning his grin into a full-on smile. And heat spreads through me, gathering in both the embarrassing and the important places.

Abracadabra.

If Matt was the Fourth of July, Noah is a summer thunderstorm, and I'm at a loss to understand why. I know that I'm suffering from a raging case of lust at first sight, but isn't that how it's supposed to start? We shouldn't just open up the boxes of our lives and dump them at each other's feet. We should lift the flaps one by one and peek inside.

"Are we headed somewhere in particular?" he asks.

"Not really," I say. "The river's just up ahead, and there's a trail along the bank. If you're interested."

"I am." He nods. "I am very interested."

With this admission, it occurs to me that Friday can mean something different for me now, too. I can lie on the log by the river with some other guy. I can kiss lips I've never kissed before. Of course, I could have reached this revelation at any moment since Justin and I broke up, but it's only now—with the possibility of kissing someone new walking along beside me—that assigning Friday a new definition seems like a step in the right direction.

"So . . . Oakland?"

"So, yeah," he says. "I was born there, but got in some trouble in high school so my mom sent me to live with my aunt and uncle in Maine. She thought it would be more . . . civilized."

Odd word choice, but I jump over it with a joke. "Kind of like the Fresh Prince in reverse."

Noah doesn't laugh, though. He just nods and says, "Something like that."

"Was your trouble the kind that leaves scars?"

"Pretty much." He runs his fingers over the pale jagged skin on his forehead. "I, uh, got hit in the head with a broken bottle."

My chest feels too tight for my lungs, and my brain wages a small battle over whether I should turn around and go back to the party. I was right about the scar, but maybe too right. "Did you . . . um . . ." Even as I try to keep my tone light, I stumble over the words. "Did you at least win the fight?"

"Shit." Noah skims his hand across the top of his head and down the back of his neck. I catch a glimpse of embarrassment in his eyes before he fixes his gaze on the ground in front of us. "I scared you. I'm sorry."

"What did you do to the other guy?"

"I don't really . . ." Noah's words just drop off, and I think he's not going to tell me. He doesn't speak for several steps, leaving the crunch of gravel and the birds to fill in the blanks. "Look, Cadie, it happened a long time ago, and this is not a story I want to tell when I'm trying to make a good first impression. I'd rather tell you who I am now."

He looks at me with maple-syrup-brown sincerity and, better judgment be damned, I believe every single word.

"You can't say something like that and then leave me hanging," I say. "I still want to know."

"I, uh . . ." He runs a hand over his head again, and his expression is so pained I almost take it back. "I broke his cheekbone with my boot."

"You kicked him in the—"

"Yeah." The word is made of quiet remorse, but my stomach still churns at the mental picture of his dusty Doc Marten turning someone's face to pulp. Boys around here get in fights, but it usually doesn't go beyond a lot of posturing and a couple of swings before someone breaks it up.

"Why would you do that?"

"I thought he was going to kill me," Noah says. "I was young and stoned and scared shitless and—I don't know—went into kind of a red rage, and when it was over, I was bleeding and he wasn't moving. One of my friends stitched me up with dental floss because I was afraid if I went to the hospital, I'd end up in jail."

I don't know how to process this. How to imagine a life in which that kind of violence is necessary. The lens through which I first saw Noah has shifted, and I don't know the right response. "Who started it?"

"Would it make a difference?"

"Maybe."

"I was defending myself." His shrug is helpless, not careless. "But that doesn't make it right."

"Well, you weren't wrong about that story."

"I shouldn't have told you. I'm sorry."

"I guess we all have history."

"Yeah? What's yours?"

"My mom died of pancreatic cancer three years ago, leaving me with a dad who is barely functioning and a baby brother I've had to raise like he's my own child," I say. "And I haven't really had a life since."

So much for lifting the flaps.

Our histories swirl in the dust that rises with our steps. The thing is, despite being unsettled by his story, I'm still attracted to Noah. Not out of some misguided bad-boy fantasy, but because I haven't been this attracted to anyone since Justin. I'm not sure what that says about me, but I want to give Noah the benefit of the doubt.

"Let's change the subject," I say, hoping he won't apologize for my mom being dead. I hate more than anything when people do that. "Socks? Cheese? Favorite board game?"

"None, Colby Jack, and the game that has the popper in the middle."

"You mean *Trouble?*"

"Oh, shit." He laughs. "Is that really what it's called?"

"It really is. But I'm more interested in your choice of identity-crisis cheese."

"There is no crisis," Noah says. "It's two cheeses in one. Double delicious."

I laugh, he smiles in a way that makes me feel as if I might not even be walking on the ground right now, and something inside me is set right again.

We've nearly reached the bend in the river, where the swing bridge spans, when the crunch of tires on the road steals up behind us. We move to the edge as Justin's truck rolls up. Gabrielle is pressed against him as he drives, and Jason hangs out the passenger window like a dog.

"Hey, Sparkles, it's skinny-dipping time," he says. "Hop in."

The bed is jammed with people, which would be dangerous if Noah and I weren't walking as fast as the truck is moving. Jason swings open the door to let me in, but I shake my head. "We'll catch up."

"I'm first come, first served."

"And I will take my chances."

"Suit yourself." The truck accelerates slightly and moves on ahead of us. Lindsey Buck waves from the tailgate where she sits with Matt, their legs dangling over the edge. His gaze lingers on me a long moment—almost too long—before he shoots a sly grin at Noah.

"That would be Matt," Noah says. "He bailed on me to chase down some girl. I guess he found her."

I could set the record straight, but what's the point? Instead, I ask why he didn't come to the party with his cousin.

He shrugs. "Campsite needed to be set up."

Justin's truck disappears around the curve, leaving us alone again.

"So what's up with the skinny-dipping?" Noah asks.

"It's a thing we do."

Because of the natural springs all over the area—which is why our town is cleverly called High Springs—the water temperature is always around seventy-two degrees. On a hot summer day like this it's going to feel really good, especially when my skin is aflame from being near Noah.

"You want to go?" he says.

"I don't know. You?"

He gives a low, slightly wicked laugh that sends electricity zipping down my spine, and I know I've got it so bad for him. "Not gonna lie, Cadie. I wouldn't turn down the opportunity to see your birthday suit."

"Then I guess today's your lucky day."

Up ahead at the river, shouts and splashes ring through the trees as everyone runs from the truck to the river, shedding their clothes on the swimming dock at the river's edge. We can't see them yet, but I've done this enough to know. Except by the time we reach the riverbank, almost everyone is already in the water, some wearing bathing suits, others not. I've never shied away from stripping off my clothes and jumping right in because I've known these people my whole life. But with Noah it's different. I've never been skinny-dipping with a stranger before.

Worse?

My bra is hanging over the shower rod in the bathroom back at home, so I can't hide behind that particular armor of cotton and lace.

With my back to Noah, I pull in a deep breath for confidence, then peel my dress up over my head. Stupid Jason catcalls that I have nice tits, so I cross my arms to hide them, hold my breath, and—leaving on my red polka-dot underwear—leap into the water. Noah splashes in beside me, and just before he drops below the surface, I catch a flash of green-plaid boxer shorts.

"Are there really gators in here?" he asks, when he comes up. We're face-to-face, only our arms and shoulders exposed as we tread water near the swimming dock. I'm hyperaware of the fact that even in the murky water Noah can see my chest, but at this point any attempt at modesty would be like shutting the barn door after the horse has escaped. Still, I kind of wish we were walking the river trail instead. Noah glances, but doesn't stare. Thankfully. "Should I worry about being eaten to death?"

Up on the bank is a yellow sign cautioning the lack of lifeguards and abundance of alligators. Just down the dock from us, Janelle Clancy sits on the edge with her feet dangling in the water because she's too afraid to go all in. Her older brother, Clay, lost a couple of fingers to a gator several years ago. Granted, he provoked the beast by being drunk, stupid, and armed with a paintball gun, but I'd probably be scared, too, if I were Janelle.

"Not really," I tell Noah. "With all the noise and thrashing around, they're going to keep their distance. But you shouldn't go swimming after dark."

"Not sure I should be swimming now."

"Don't worry." It feels like we're in our own little

bubble as I smile at him. I can't seem to stop smiling at him. "I'll protect you."

"You're not like one of those swamp girls on TV who kiss alligators on the mouth, are you?"

"No." I stare at Noah's lips and wrestle with how shocking my own behavior is right now. But, God, I want to kiss him so badly. "Not gators."

Like he's reading my mind, he moves toward me in the water and touches his lips to mine. But trying to kiss someone and stay afloat in twelve feet of water—at the same time—is complicated. We keep kicking each other's legs and our mouths won't stay together, and finally we're just laughing too hard to even bother.

"Maybe we should try again on dry land," Noah suggests.

"Definitely."

His eyebrows rise. "Soon?"

"Yes."

"Now?"

We haven't been in the water long enough to even count it as swimming, but there's only one answer. "Yes."

Noah climbs the swim ladder first and goes over to our pile of discarded clothes. Aside from his tattoo sleeves, the rest of his body—except the bit I can't see because it's covered by saggy wet boxer shorts—is tattoo-free. Lean, but not skinny. Tight with muscles.

"Hey, Sparkles, looking for this?" Jason, his tighty-whities wet, practically transparent, and completely gross, stands on the dock holding my dress.

"Just give it to Noah, please."

"Come get it." He twirls it above his head like a lasso.

"Jason, please."

Justin swims past me and climbs up the ladder onto the dock.

"Why so shy, Cadie?" Jason says. "It's not like we all haven't seen you naked before."

My face catches fire, and I hate the way he makes it sound like a dirty thing. I don't look around for fear every-one is staring at me, and I don't look at Noah for fear of what I might see written on his face. Now I really wish I were at home in my pajamas with Daniel Boone. Or anywhere other than here.

"Because every other time we've been swimming I've been able to get out of the water and put on my clothes," I say, with a lot more courage than I feel. "But right now, Jason, I don't have that option. I have to stay naked until you feel like giving my dress back and, quite frankly, that's kind of rape-y."

"Jesus Christ, Arcadia." He says my name like it's a disease, his voice loud, angry, and echoing through the trees, making me wonder if the whole state park can hear him. "I'm not a rapist. Don't even joke about shit like that."

"Give her back the dress"—Noah's voice is hard, and the fingers of his right hand keep clenching in and out of a fist—"or I will fuck you up." At the same time he threatens Jason with bodily harm, Justin steps up beside Noah, forming an uneven wall of defense between Jason and me. Justin says his brother's name like a one-word warning.

"Fine."

I don't know whether Jason is giving in to Noah or Justin, but his eyes are on mine—his mouth curled into his trademark smirk—as he throws my dress into the river.

CHAPTER 4

Holding the sodden fabric to my chest, I climb the ladder and walk up the ramp with all the dignity I have left, which isn't very much. Water drips off the end of my hair into my eyes, but I don't wipe it away because I don't want anyone to mistake it for crying.

"What the hell were you thinking?" Justin demands of his brother, but Noah calls my name, blotting out Jason's answer.

"Wait a sec." Noah catches up with me at the top of the ramp, offering his T-shirt. "Here. It's dry." He turns around without my having to ask—a sweetness that makes my chest ache—and waits while I wring the excess water from my hair and pull on his sun-warmed shirt.

"Thanks," I say, when I'm as pulled together as I'm going to get, and he turns to face me. Lifting to my toes, I reach up and curve my hand around the back of his neck. His skin is cool from the river, and I can feel his pulse thumping beneath my thumb—as crazy fast as mine, I think—as I touch my lips against his. I kiss him once. His mouth is so gentle that my brain slips out of focus.

Twice. His hands are on my face, and his tongue grazes mine.

A third time. Stars are born, while others wink out of existence as we kiss, so I'm surprised when I open my eyes and find time has barely passed at all.

"I could kick his ass," he whispers, our lips so close they brush as he says the words. Between kisses. Because now that we've started in earnest, it feels too good to stop. Two years with Justin, and I've never, ever been kissed like this.

"You could," I say. "But I'd rather fight my own battles. I don't need to be rescued. I do appreciate the shirt, though."

Lindsey runs up, her dirty-blond hair and green-striped bikini dripping wet from the river, and offers me a pair of denim shorts. "I brought spares," she explains. "If you, um . . . if you want to borrow them."

I accept because she and I are about the same size, but

what is more important, her spare shorts are dry and my underwear is not. And I hate wearing wet underwear. "Thanks, Lindsey."

"Jason is such an"—she leans in close and her little bell voice goes so soft I can barely hear her—"asshole."

My eyes go wide with shock. Lindsey's brothers practically wrote the book on profanity, but I've never once heard her swear. Not even shined-up substitutes like "fudge" or "dang it." Hearing her call Jason Kendrick an asshole is monumental. And the word sounds so funny coming out of her mouth that it takes everything in me not to crack up laughing. Before I can agree, she scurries back down to the swim dock, leaving a trail of wet footprints opposite the ones she made coming up, and plunges into the river.

Jason shook me off like water and is now organizing a cannonball competition, while Justin stands down on the dock looking up at me as if I'm someone he's never seen before. I turn away and shrink inside the comforting bigness of Noah's shirt to wiggle out of my wet underwear and pull on Lindsey's shorts, feeling as if I'm in the grade school locker room all over again. So much for beautiful and dangerous.

Arcadia Wells. Soggy. Embarrassed.

Except Noah's big hand swallows up my own, and all the wild feelings come flooding back until they fill me again. "So," he says. "What do you say we get the hell out of here?"

"I'd like that more than anything."

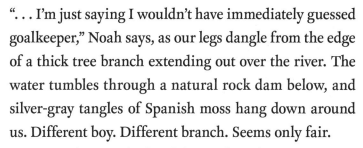

". . . I'm just saying I wouldn't have immediately guessed goalkeeper," Noah says, as our legs dangle from the edge of a thick tree branch extending out over the river. The water tumbles through a natural rock dam below, and silver-gray tangles of Spanish moss hang down around us. Different boy. Different branch. Seems only fair.

We're sharing the headphones from his iPod, so one ear is getting the slide of a ska trombone and the other is hearing the dancing song of the river. My voice is worn thin from talking. Trading bits of our lives. His absentee dad for my going through chemotherapy with Mom. His street kid childhood for my imaginary world tour. His magna cum laude degree in wildlife management for my thoroughly unimpressive 57th in a graduating class of 314. I learn that Noah inherited the '69 Cougar from his recently deceased Savannah grandmother. And that it does, indeed, have the original 351. He hears about my secret wardrobe and how I like to repurpose thrift store church-lady dresses. We collect each other's stories like a game of Go Fish, swapping until we have a match and our hands are full. Until the sun is about to slip below the horizon. It's been so long since I've really talked with someone. Felt so present in my own life.

"Really," I say. "Why do I not seem like a goalkeeper?"

"Seems like you bring the fight rather than waiting for it to come to you," he says. "So—I don't know—I figured you for a striker."

I turn the idea over in my mind a few times and decide I'm pleased with his answer. We fall silent for a moment, and the unrelenting sound of the night insects seems to consume the air around us. Noah slaps at his bare forearm, and I dig the bottle of bug lotion from my knapsack. "I was a fullback," he says. "Usually center, but sometimes left."

"Any good?"

"Not a contender for the MLS, but not bad. You?"

I shrug. "I'd have liked the chance to get better."

"You miss it?" he asks.

"All the time."

"Me, too." Noah shifts himself from sitting to standing, balancing carefully on the branch, then extends a hand to help me up. "Do you think you'll be sticking around tonight? I brought a ball, so if you want to stay, we could maybe kick it around tomorrow."

By now Duane is probably settled in, watching a movie with Jess, so I don't want to bother him. I could probably catch a ride with someone heading back to town yet tonight, but there are plenty of reasons I don't want to go home. The biggest one is standing in front of me. "I'll stay."

Noah reaches for my other hand and brings them both up around his neck. "Good," he says, just before his lips graze mine. Goose bumps follow his hands down my arms, my sides, back to my waist. We balance there on the tree, kissing until it's too dark to see—and beyond, now that we've learned each other's mouths by heart.

I find the flashlight at the bottom of my bag as we make our way back to the Magnolia loop. Playing the beam along the path, I search out cypress knees that might trip us up, and Noah moves behind me when scrubby palms squeeze us into single file. He lets go of my hand then, but only until the trail spreads wide again and we can walk side by side. Which is good, because I like the feel of his palm against mine.

When we finally reach the campsite, deep twilight has descended and the party has swollen with people and the music is loud enough to attract the attention of the park rangers. Jason and a few others—including Matt and Lindsey—are gathered by the beer trough doing Jell-O shots. Matt waves in our direction, but my eyes move on, seeking out Justin. He's toasting marshmallows over the fire with Gabrielle.

"Beer?" Noah asks me, as he sends a two-fingered wave back to his cousin.

I shake my head. "I'm good."

"Hungry?"

I'd really love to make s'mores with Noah, but it would feel weird. Like I was trying too hard to show Justin that I'm okay without him, even though I really *am* okay without him. I hate that my present is rubbing up against my past. "I'd take a hot dog if there are any left."

"Condiments?"

"Surprise me."

I sit on the end of an adjustable beach chair opposite Justin and try not to watch him feed Gabrielle a gooey marshmallow and remember how she used to be me. How he would kiss me afterward so he could taste the sweetness in my mouth.

Impossible.

Instead, I lie back and search for shooting stars— maybe the one that will shoot me right out of this town— until my ex-boyfriend and his girlfriend and the party itself fade to background noise. Until Noah's face appears over me with his better-than-a-shooting-star smile and I am reminded why I stayed.

"Sit up." He positions himself behind me on the chair so I'm between his legs with my back against his chest as we inhale chili dogs with ketchup like we haven't eaten for days. We share a can of Coke and a secret smile over our gluttony, and after I finish licking the last of the chili off my fingertips, Noah kisses me. It's the kind of kiss that

makes me want to roll beneath him. Feel the weight of
him pressing down against me. It scares me because for
all the talking we did at the river, he's still a stranger. But
this wanting is burning me up, and I don't know what to
do about it.

"We could go back to my campsite." His voice is low
and shivery beside my ear, and a rash of goose bumps
spreads across the backs of my thighs.

I glance across the fire to check on Justin and Gabrielle, but they have been replaced by Matt and Lindsey,
who have moved from Jell-O shots and flirty smiles to
full-on making out. And it hits me that my presence at
this party doesn't affect Justin at all. He doesn't care
what I'm eating or who I'm kissing. And checking out
my ass isn't the same as wanting me back. I've ensnared
myself in my own stupid, imaginary drama. I look at
Noah. "Let's go."

"Hey, Sparkles!" Jason calls with a liquid tongue as
we leave. "Wait."

Maybe he means to apologize but I don't answer and
I don't look back. With Noah's fingers threaded through
mine we practically run to his campsite, where my dress—
that he brought here before our walk—billows softly from
a thin clothesline strung between tall oaks. I'm already
half-mad for him and seeing the way he hung the dress
with such care sends me completely over the edge.

"This is me." Noah releases my hand to unzip the flap

on one of two dome tents, and we duck through the entrance. He switches on a small battery-operated lantern and pulls me down with him onto a double-size air mattress covered by a green sleeping bag and an old grandmotherly-looking quilt. We kiss each other the same way we ate the chili dogs. Hungry. Fast. His hand burrows beneath my shirt, as my own hands slide up his broad, warm back. His hip bones press into mine, and when his hand covers my breast, I don't push it away.

There are no sweet words whispered in the dark. No words at all. Just mouths and hands and peeled-back layers until we're clothed in nothing but the scent of the river that clings to our skin. It's only then I realize I'm on the brink of having sex with a stranger and that we need to have a conversation about protection. Or maybe about the fact that I'm not sure I want to do this. "Noah, wait. Stop."

"Right." He breathes the word against my neck. "Condoms. We need condoms." He sits up and looks around as if he's a little disoriented. I understand, because I've been feeling upside-down since I met him. "I have condoms."

"No, I mean—" I sit up and pull my knees against my chest. "I can't do this."

"Oh."

"I like you. I really, really do, but I barely even know

you. Maybe you and Matt hook up with girls at every campground, and that's okay. It's totally not my business." I know I'm babbling, but I can't stop myself. "But I feel completely out of control around you and it scares me, and I'm not sure I'm the kind of girl who can just do this."

He snatches his boxer shorts off the tent floor with a frustrated snap. "I just don't—" He blows out a breath, unzips the entrance flap, and steps outside. "I need some air."

CHAPTER 5

I get dressed and wait a few minutes, wondering if Noah is coming back—and whether I want to be here when he does. The last time I turned Justin down for sex, he got all sulky and accused me of being a tease. He claimed he was only joking, but it made me feel unnecessarily guilty and we ended up fighting. I might be able to forgive Noah's past, but not respecting my right to say no is a deal breaker.

Except I am distracted by a copy of John Steinbeck's *Travels with Charley*—a whitened seam from multiple readings running down its faded orange spine—lying face-down beside the air mattress. I have too many favorite books to commit to a short list, but if I had one, this book would be on it. *The Grapes of Wrath* put me off Steinbeck after reading it for American Lit, but Mr. Dean bet me five dollars that *Travels with Charley* would win me back.

I pick up Noah's copy to see what page he's on. Beneath the book is a brown leather wallet, which is infinitely more irresistible than Steinbeck. Inside there's some cash, a debit card, a Maine driver's license, and a student ID from the University of Maine. But, even more interesting to a word nerd like me, is that Noah Thomas MacNeal, age twenty-two, has two library cards—one from Oakland and one from a library called Jesup in Bar Harbor, Maine. I don't know why, but this knowledge makes me smile.

I place the wallet back in its hiding place and go out to fetch my dress off the clothesline. The fabric is stiff from drying, and it doesn't smell much better than I do, but I put it on over Lindsey's shorts. I'm folding Noah's T-shirt when he comes back through the flap dressed in only boxers and unlaced boots, and trailed by an Australian cattle dog with a patchwork muzzle.

"Hi," I say, watching his face for an expression I can recognize.

"Hey."

"Trading one bitch for another?" I say it like a joke—even if I'm not sure it is—and Noah's serious mouth curves into a smile. He lowers himself to sit on the air mattress beside me. "I guess I owe you another apology," he says. "I thought you were into it, so you kind of took me by surprise when you put on the brakes and— I shouldn't have stomped off like an asshole."

The dog rests her head on my knee—I know she's a she because the name Molly is engraved on the bone-shaped tag on her collar—and I stroke the soft fur between her pointy ears. "Apology accepted," I say. "And just so you know, I was totally into it until—well, until I wasn't. You didn't do anything wrong. I just got cold feet, and I appreciate you stopping when I asked."

"Why wouldn't I stop? I'm not a complete Neander-thal."

"You're not even a little bit."

"Yeah, well, I wouldn't be so sure about that," he says. "But if it's any consolation, I don't make a habit of picking up random girls at campgrounds. I saw you walking down the road in that dress looking like you owned the world, and I just wanted to know you. I still do, but we're gonna have to do it with our clothes on because you make me crazy, too."

I lean over and kiss his cheek, then gather up the grandma quilt. "So where have you been hiding this sweet girl?"

"She's been crashed out in Matt's tent," he says, reach-ing down to scratch the dog's cheek, and I'd swear to God she is smiling at him. "Her name is Molly, and I picked her up last summer at a farm stand up in Maine. They were selling blueberries and puppies. I stopped for the berries, and ended up with the best damn dog in the world."

"She's beautiful." I take the quilt outside to spread it beside the fire pit. Molly follows.

"More importantly, she's brilliant," Noah says, and I like that he prefers brains over beauty, even if he's talking about his dog. A few moments later he emerges from the tent, this time with all his clothes on. "Come morning, I'll show you everything she can do."

He stacks some firewood in the pit. The fire catches, and we lie on the ground with our faces tilted skyward. Molly settles warm against my side. Flare-ups of laughter tell me the party is still going strong down the way, but this is so much better.

"Is your name really Arcadia?" Noah asks.

"Yep."

"Why?"

"I have no idea." I tell him about Mom's baby name book and my theory about her wanting an adventurous life for me. "But new baby name books say it means unspoiled paradise, so maybe that blows my theory all to hell."

"Or maybe it means your mom looked at you and saw something unspoiled and perfect."

It sounds like a really smooth pickup line, but it causes an unexpected sadness to catch in my chest, and the stars turn into a Van Gogh sky as my eyes sting with tears. I blink until they recede. "I've never thought about it like that."

Noah inches closer to me and shifts his arm so I can rest my head against his chest. He doesn't smell like citrus or a pine forest or any of those things boys smell like in books. There's only the faint scent of sweat and a stronger note of wood smoke that makes me want to climb inside his skin. He smells like someone real, and his heart travels through bone and blood, skin and cotton, to beat against my cheek. "Maybe," he says, "you should."

I'm afraid talking about my mom will make me cry, because that still happens once in a while, so I ask if his tattoos hurt and he tells me they didn't. Then I ask if he's sick of that question. "That one and the one wanting to know what they all mean."

"Do they mean anything?"

"Not really," he says. "I've always been a big fan of old-school Sailor Jerry–style ink, but the only reason I got this one"—he points to a schooner riding the crest of a wave—"was to cover up a shitty stick-and-poke tattoo I did myself. Then I just kept getting more."

I run my fingertips along his arm, but it doesn't feel any different covered with ink. Not that I thought it would. My fingers reach Noah's wrist, and I touch the circle of wooden beads around it. "What's this?"

"It's called a mala," he says. "A string of Buddhist prayer beads."

"Are you Buddhist?"

Most everyone around High Springs is some form of Christian, mostly Southern Baptist. Mom was Methodist so we were all Methodist, but we're not much of anything anymore. Sometimes I worry about Daniel Boone missing out on Sunday school and the beauty of the church filled with redemption and white lilies on Easter morning, and I know Mom would want me to take him. But going to church is just too hard without her.

I don't know any non-Christians.

"I'm agnostic, I guess, but I got it from a punk-rock Buddhist monk back home who thought meditation might help me get my shit together," Noah explains. "I suck at meditating because when things get quiet, my brain tends to dredge up random song lyrics and all the stupid shit I've ever done, but I keep the mala as a reminder that nothing is permanent. Anger passes. Stupidity is usually temporary. And even the best things in life can't last forever."

"Does it work?" I ask, wondering if something like that would make getting from one day to the next any easier.

His laugh is quiet, and I can feel his lips against my temple as he answers. "Most of the time it's just a string of beads."

Noah laces his fingers with mine, and we don't talk. In the quiet, the noise of the party drifts our way a couple of times. The forest undergrowth crackles around us. A faraway plane tricks me into thinking it's a shooting star. My eyes get heavy, and I'm on the edge of sleep when Molly's head perks up, her ears like little radar receivers, at the sound of a sharp, strange birdcall. At least it's no bird I've ever heard around here. Noah whistles back a matching call.

"Matt," he explains, as his cousin and Lindsey emerge from the darkness into the firelight. Noah lifts his head. "Hey, guys."

"Don't you two just look all cozy?" Matt says.

"Don't we just?" Noah replies, making no move to change position.

Matt adds a fat log to the fire, sending up a burst of orange sparks, as Lindsey parks herself on the corner of the quilt near my feet. Even though I'd rather stay right here with my head against Noah's shoulder, I sit up to make more room for her.

Lindsey and I used to spend whole recess periods back in elementary school drawing elaborate chalk cities on the blacktop, but when we got to middle school I joined the soccer team while she hung out with the smart kids. Now we're friendly enough that it's not weird to be wearing her shorts, but we don't have much in common anymore.

"How was the party?" I ask.

She shrugs. "Park rangers will probably be around shortly to bust things up because some old people in an RV complained about the music being too loud."

"Typical."

Matt finishes stoking the fire, and the blanket gets even more crowded. In the firelight his skin turns golden, and even after a swim in the river his hair looks clean and soft. He catches me checking him out and smirks as I look away.

"Cadie, this is my cousin, Matt," Noah says. "Matt, this is—"

"The infamous Arcadia Wells," Matt interrupts. "I know. We've met. At the ranger station, if you want to get technical about it."

"Wait. Is she—" I can almost see the lightbulb switch on over Noah's head as he realizes it wasn't Lindsey who invited Matt to the campfire party. "Oh, shit. Sorry, dude. Didn't mean to poach."

"Poach?" My eyebrows practically climb up into my hairline. "Seriously? Like, I'm an endangered white rhino instead of a person? Pretty sure I'm capable of choosing for myself, instead of waiting around for you guys to decide who gets me. So that's not what you meant by poach, right?"

In the awkward silence that follows, I wonder if I'm overreacting. My mother nurtured strong opinions in me, and sometimes I think they push people away. But why should I have to change who I am so someone else will like me? Why should anyone have to do that? And why shouldn't I call boys out on their bullshit?

Noah's pinkie finger brushes against mine on the blanket. "I'm sorry, Cadie."

The soulful sound of my name coming from his mouth makes me want to forgive him on the spot. I don't want to be mad tonight. I'm away from home, free from every little responsibility that holds me down, and sitting beside me is a guy I want to kiss again very soon. I reach my arm into the cooler and fish out a couple of icy cans. "Who wants a beer?"

After I distribute a round, the mood seems to click back to normal and we sit for a while, discussing the guys' plan to end their camping trip at Flamingo. According to Matt, the residents were relocated after Hurricane Wilma and the town became part of Everglades National Park.

"There are streets with no houses," he explains. "Just the concrete pads where the houses once stood."

I smile. "Sounds like the perfect kind of creepy."

"Exactly," he says, smiling back as if we're together on some inside joke. "But I also think we should go to Disney World."

Noah casts a skeptical eye at him. "You were the one

who said we should stick to camping and skip the tourist stuff."

"Yeah, but it'll be fun," Matt insists. He drops his arm around Lindsey's shoulder. "Especially if we convince a couple of pretty girls to go with us."

Lindsey giggles, her eyes shining with hope, and I'm not sure if she's more excited about the idea of spending more time with Matt or going to the Magic Kingdom.

The first time my parents took me to Disney World, I was six. My memories are pretty vague, except that my dad spent the extra money for tickets to Epcot Center just because the only Disney character I wanted to meet was Mulan and she was at Epcot. And I remember getting sick after riding the teacups. Our class went to Disney at the end of seventh grade, too, but now that I think about it, Lindsey didn't go.

"Dude," Noah says, his voice low. "I thought we weren't."

There's something in his tone that leaves me wondering if they're still talking about Disney World, and the air feels thick with whatever is not being said, but Matt laughs it away. "Cadie might like the teacup ride."

"Don't count on it," I say. "Last time I rode those things, I puked orange soda all over my mom's legs."

"I think . . ." Noah gets to his feet and offers me a hand up. "Maybe we should talk about this in the morning."

I say good night to Matt and Lindsey as Noah stalks off toward his tent, leaving Molly and a very confused me to catch up. "So what was that about?" I ask, when we're zipped up inside.

"Every summer since I moved to Maine, Matt and I have done a trip," he says. "One year we hiked the two-hundred-and-eighty-one-mile section of the Appalachian Trail that runs up through Maine. Another year we paddled the coastline from Kittery to Calais. This is probably our last summer, so we agreed it was just going to be us, you know?"

I nod. "It's a good plan."

"It was," Noah says. "Until I met you, and I thought about how cool it would be if you came with us. But I wasn't going to ask because of the agreement. Only now he's invited Lindsey to go to Disney World?"

"Maybe he really likes her."

"He likes *you*."

"Now you're just being crazy," I say. "Matt doesn't even know me. And besides, if I was going to run off to Disney World with a stranger, it would be you."

He smiles as he reaches for me, and I can feel the warmth of his hands through the thin fabric of my dress. He kisses me dizzy, then whispers in my ear, "Want to run off with me?"

The whole idea is insane, but part of me wants to say

yes. The part of me that can picture holding his free hand while he drives. Kissing at red lights in one-intersection towns. Sleeping on an air mattress with an Australian cattle dog named Molly. The part of me that's been waiting for an adventure my whole life.

"Ask me again tomorrow." I lie down on his mattress, and Noah spoons up behind me as his dog curls against my stomach. I smile. What's more likely to happen tomorrow is, I'll go home and spend the day with Daniel Boone and a basket of dirty laundry. But tonight . . . this imperfectly perfect night will be pressed in my memory the way Mom pressed flowers between the pages of the dusty old dictionary.

"I shouldn't," he says, his voice heavy with sleep. "But I will."

The morning sky is the kind Daniel Boone calls "sheepy"—pale blue pasture filled with pink and purple puffs that look like a close-together flock of sheep—when I wake up needing to use the bathroom. Also, feeling shy because I've never woken up with a guy after an entire night together. Justin would sometimes fall asleep with me on my bed, but only just until his curfew. I have no idea what time it is as I wiggle out from under Noah's arm and push my feet into my boots. Molly follows me to the entrance flap, but when I whisper that I'll be right back, she hops up on the mattress beside Noah.

Matt is standing outside his tent. He's still wearing last night's clothes, and his hair is scruffy and more than a little bit sexy. My own hair is beyond dirty. After sleep and river water, I'm afraid to even look at it.

"You're up early," he says.

"Occupational hazard," I say. "I have a little brother who thinks six a.m. is a reasonable time of day. I'm heading to the bathroom. You?"

"Same. I'll walk with you. How old is your brother?"

"Almost four."

"My little sister, Lily, just turned five," he says. "She was, um—unexpected."

I nod. "Danny was an oops baby, too, but I can't even imagine what life would be like without him."

"Lily's pretty adorable," Matt says. "She used to wear these star-shaped sunglasses and tell me she was a movie star, only she said 'moobie.' Cracked me up every time."

My brother is probably up already, and I wonder if Dad's handling the morning routine okay. It's not as if they've never been alone together, but not usually overnight, and I don't trust Dad to make the eggs right. I can't even remember a morning I haven't been there. My phone is in my knapsack back in Noah's tent, so I can't call to check in.

"What are you guys doing today?" I ask.

"The plan is to do some paddling on the Santa Fe River and then spend another night," he says. "But we need to head to town for some groceries."

"That works out kind of perfectly because I need to get to town and my dad owns a grocery store," I say. "So if you'll drop me off, I'll get you the family discount."

"You're not sticking around?" Matt asks, as we come up on the Kendrick brothers' campsite. "I was serious about the Disney thing. I mean, Noah hates the idea, but Lindsey seems stoked."

People are crashed out in sleeping bags and in the back of pickup trucks, and Justin's parents' pop-up camper is popped at the back of the site. I kick a beer can, scattering the little plastic Jell-O shot cups that litter the ground.

"Yeah, I don't think she's ever . . ." My words trail off when I see Jason propped naked against a big oak. It's not completely unreasonable for him to get drunk and take off his clothes, but on second glance it looks as if he's *tied* in place. "What the hell?"

There's a slash of silver duct tape across his mouth. A clothesline, wrapped several times around the trunk, holds him against the tree. As I kneel in the dirt beside him trying to untie him, I can see his body is covered with insect bites. Big puffy pink ones from mosquitoes. Tiny red pinpoints made by no-see-ums. And the angry blister bubbles left by red ants. There are even a couple of ticks in the forest of hair on his arms. I don't even want to think about the other places he may have suffered bites.

Matt unfolds a camp knife and moves behind the tree to cut the rope as I lift Jason's head. "God, Kendrick, you big dumb hick," I say, trying to keep from crying. "What did you do?"

I pick carefully at the corner of the tape, and Jason's eyelids fly open so suddenly I nearly jump clean out of my skin. My heart is racing as he makes muffled sounds at me, his eyes desperate and wild. "Let me just—"

Matt reaches down and rips away the duct tape fast, taking a bit of skin from Jason's lower lip and leaving a bloody patch in its place. Jason yelps in pain and covers his mouth with dirty hands.

"Jesus, Matt, why did you do that?" I know it's too early in the morning for shouting, but I can't help myself.

"It would have hurt more doing it your way," he says, pulling a blanket out from under Sammy Presley and throwing it over Jason. "What happened?"

"I don't know." Tears cut tracks in the grime as they trickle down Jason's face, and he's crying the way Daniel Boone gets when he can't stop. Ragged. Choking. My cheeks burn with embarrassment for Jason, especially when people around us are waking up and he's an entirely different boy than the one we all know. Matt steps away to phone for help.

"I can't remember. I just—the ants kept biting me."
Jason dry-heaves, and the tears keep coming. My heart
breaks a little to see him like this. "I tried to call for help,
but no one could hear me."

"An ambulance is on the way." Matt gently squeezes
my shoulder as I rub Jason's back through the blanket,
assuring him over and over that everything will be okay.
Everyone is awake now, and Justin comes over, squatting
down beside his brother.

"Who did this?" Justin asks, but Jason shakes his
head.

"I don't know. I did some Jell-O shots and then . . . I
can't remember anything." He goes quiet for a moment,
then looks up at me and gives me a little smile that's
half-sad, half-regular Jason. He wipes his face with
his oversize LEGO-block hand, streaking more dirt
across his forehead. "Please, Sparkles, tell me we had sex."

"You stupid jerk," I say, but inside I'm relieved he's
going to be okay.

CHAPTER 6

The ambulance arrives with no lights or sirens, but a crowd, made up of campers from around the loop, still gathers. Jason's ego has been kicked around plenty for one day, and the last thing he needs is an audience, but he's in pretty bad shape. The EMTs decide his bites should be seen by a doctor, but they don't put Jason on a gurney or anything like that. He just climbs down from the picnic table where we've been waiting together.

"Hey, um, Cadie," he says, tightening the pink floral blanket around him as he looks at the ground and then up at me. His eyes are rimmed red, and the spot on his lip has turned dark where the bleeding has stopped. "I'm sorry about your dress."

"I don't even know what you're talking about," I say,

and a smile breaks through the dirt on his face as he steps up into the back of the ambulance.

"See ya, Sparkles." The doors close behind him, and a minute later they drive off, leaving the rest of us wondering what exactly happened. Speculating on how Jason ended up tied to a tree and who might have done it. Except no one saw it happen, and now that he is gone, Chris Gannon and Sammy, both of thick neck and small brain, start snickering behind their hands like a pair of kindergarteners.

"Did you guys do this?" I gesture toward the oak, where the clothesline is puddled at the base and the imprint of Jason's backside is pressed in the dirt. "Because it's not remotely funny."

"Dude, no," Chris protests. "I was passed out in the back of Kendrick's truck, but come on, Cadie, he had it coming. You have to admit it's kind of hilarious."

Only it's not, because when Matt tore off the duct tape, I could smell the vomit on Jason's breath. He'd gotten so hysterical in the night he'd thrown up in his own mouth and couldn't do anything but swallow it. My eyes burn, and I have to count to ten so I won't say something terrible. Even then, what I do say is not very nice. "You guys are such dicks."

The park rangers move through the people at the campsite, asking questions about what happened. Even though they're local guys—which is why they typically just break up our campfire parties instead of arresting us—they still have to do their jobs. Everyone buttons up, though, not wanting to get in trouble for underage drinking. Every single person at the campsite, including me, denies tying Jason Kendrick to a tree. Most of us aren't lying when we say we have no idea, but someone is.

My bladder has just about reached critical mass when the rangers let me go. I'm halfway to the bathroom when Justin catches up with me on the road. "Hey, Cadie," he says. "Thanks for taking care of my brother. You are, um— I miss you."

For months after he broke up with me I'd have given everything to hear those words come out of his mouth and to see him standing in front of me with his eyes all soft and sweet. But not today.

"Do you really? Or is it because you saw me kissing another guy?" I say. "Because now is the wrong time to be talking about this. You could have called me two months ago or maybe—maybe you could have not dumped me. What I did for Jason is what any decent human being should do. It wasn't about you. And—I just really need to pee, so you should go back to your girlfriend and pretend we never had this conversation."

I don't wait around for Justin's reply.

Matt comes out of the bathroom building just as I get there, and he waits outside while I take a hobo bath in the sink using paper towels and pink liquid hand soap. Face. Chest. Underarms. Girl bits. It doesn't really help because my dress is smeared with Jason's snot and tears, and I hate wearing denim shorts without underwear, but at least I'm a little less grungy.

"So that was a bizarre start to the day," Matt says, as we head back to the campsite. "You doing all right?"

"I think so, yeah," I say. "I mean, who would do something like that?"

Around here we all know the stupid pranks Jason Kendrick pulls don't mean anything. He's a harmless goofball. A clown. And, really, if anyone had been out for revenge last night, it would have been me. Except I would never do that because I love Jason like an annoying brother. He drives me crazy, but never to the point of revenge.

"Maybe it was a prank that got out of hand," Matt says. "Or payback. You can't tell me that of everyone at the party last night, there aren't a few of them who'd like to tie him to a tree."

I want to defend Jason, but there's probably a waiting list of volunteers. "I guess you're right. Yesterday I'd have been one of them."

"So would his brother."

"No way." The idea is so absurd I have to shake my head. "Jason was basically tortured last night. Justin would never do that."

Matt shrugs. "Everyone has their breaking point, Cadie. Maybe he humiliated Jason as punishment for embarrassing you."

"No. I don't believe that."

He doesn't say anything more, so I change the subject. "Even after a wash, I still feel pretty gross. I'm ready to go home and shower."

"Does this mean you're not going to Disney World with us?"

"Haven't decided yet," I say. "But if I'm hanging out with you guys today, I need a change of clothes."

Matt smiles, and the rabble of butterflies that seem to have taken up residence in my stomach since I met these boys from Maine go on a fluttering spree. My mind travels back to last night, to what Noah said about Matt liking me. My skin doesn't feel crowded to near-bursting the way it does when I'm around Noah, and maybe if I'd stuck around at the party with Matt . . . I don't know. Maybe.

"Thanks for helping me this morning," I say.

"It was the least I could do." The wattage on Matt's smile amps up, and the butterflies do another crazy little dance. "So maybe you know this already," he says. "But

Bar Harbor, where we live in Maine, is part of a national park called Acadia."

"I've heard of it."

"What you might not know is that back in the sixteenth century it was a much larger area that included parts of Canada and was named Arcadia because it was considered an unspoiled wilderness, a kind of utopia. Later, the French dropped the letter *r* and it became Acadia."

"I didn't know that part." The geography nerd in me loves this trivial tidbit of information, especially since it relates to my name, and I can't say I'm not a little charmed. "Acadia, huh?"

"Yep," he says. "The sunsets there are some of the best, especially when the sky turns red over Cadillac Mountain. "You should see it."

"I'm adding it to my mental to-visit list as we speak."

"Put Disney World on the list, too," Matt says as we reach the campsite. "Because I really hope you'll come with us."

Noah sits on a log beside the fire, drinking coffee out of a blue-speckled camp mug and prodding at the smoldering wood with a stick. Lindsey is hunched over her own steaming mug at the other end of the log, her hair tangled around her shoulders. She looks tired, and it occurs to me that it's still really early. Barely seven.

"Hey." Noah hands me his mug as I sit down beside him. I take a sip, then hand it back. Our shoulders and upper arms press together as if they're made of Velcro, and I want to kiss his sleepy face. "Where ya been?"

I tell him about Jason.

"That's some messed-up shit," Noah says. "Any idea who did it?"

"No one's talking."

"My money's still on the brother." Matt pours himself some coffee. "He didn't look happy when you two left the party last night." He gestures toward Noah and me with his mug. "And he was pretty pissed off at the river yesterday."

"So was Noah." Lindsey's face turns pink when all three of us look at her. "I didn't mean—oh my God, I'm sorry. I don't mean you would do that. I meant that I don't think Noah or Justin would hurt Jason."

"I wouldn't." There's a sharp edge to Noah's denial. "I didn't."

Still, I think about the way his fist curled and uncurled as he stood on the dock yesterday. Like he really wanted to hit Jason.

"Cadie." The quiet way Noah says my name makes me turn in his direction. He looks me in the eye and says the words again. "I didn't."

He was with me all night in the tent, and I woke with

his tattooed arm curled around me, the same way it was when we fell asleep. There were dents on my skin this morning from where the wooden mala beads pressed against my arm. Molly would have stirred and tried to follow him. I would have felt the wobbly mattress shift if he left, wouldn't I?

"Have we considered that he might have accidentally tangled himself up?" Noah asks, echoing my initial thoughts when I first discovered Jason.

"Totally plausible." Lindsey giggles, because she knows that tying himself to a tree is within Jason's wheelhouse of stupid.

Except the rope was wrapped too tight, too neatly, for him to have done it himself. And knotted at the back of the tree where he couldn't have reached. Not to mention the duct tape on his mouth. It couldn't have been an accident.

"Well, it wasn't one of us because we were all here together," Matt says. "And since the paramedics said your friend will be okay, why don't we head into town, grab some breakfast, and then do something fun. Lindsey, are you in?"

"Definitely." Her face shines with adoration as she nods, making me wonder exactly what the two of them were doing last night while Noah and I were sleeping. Not that it's any of my business, but I'm curious.

"Cadie?" Matt directs the same question at me, and I snap back to reality.

Dad's going to be expecting me at home—even though it is Rhea Chung's morning to open the store and he doesn't have to go in until two—but I'm not ready for this to be over yet. "I'm in."

"This is it." I lean between the front bucket seats, between Noah and Matt, and point to my house. Noah parks the Cougar in our empty driveway—strange, considering the early hour—and they all follow me to the front door, including Molly, who pauses to squat on the lawn. Her back half practically disappears in the embarrassing grass. Viewed through the eyes of a pair of well-off strangers, yesterday's shabbiness seems even worse. I notice the dirt around the doorknob we touch every day. How the bottom of one of the wooden roof supports has broken off. One of Uncle Eddie's cigarette butts, smashed out among the overgrown hibiscus shrubs, glares at me like neon. I don't even know if Matt and Noah see these things, but I can't unnotice them, and I wonder if they think of me as some kind of white-trash girl.

Inside is better. I vacuumed a couple of days ago, there are no dirty dishes in the sink, and the door to the laundry room is closed, so they can't see the mountain of clothes on top of the dryer. I find a sticky note on the refrigerator door from my dad, telling me he took Daniel Boone—it makes me smile that he actually wrote Daniel Boone instead of Danny—to the IHOP up in Lake City for pancakes and that I should enjoy my day off. Not sure what happened to make Dad's attitude do a one-eighty, but I'm not questioning it.

Matt and Lindsey hang out in the living room, looking at the collection of artwork hanging above the couch. Mom dabbled in photography, so there are some black-and-whites of me and of Dad, and even one when my brother was learning to crawl and she was getting too sick to take pictures. There's my first painting of a trio of red and yellow tulips, and a scribble Danny made with chunky crayons before he could talk. And a framed Charley Harper print of an opossum mother carrying her babies on her back that's actually a page from an old calendar. I think possums are satanic fur-covered skeletons, but my mom thought they were crazy adorable.

Noah follows me into my room.

"So this is where the magic happens, huh?" The ordinarily normal-size space seems so small around him as he sits on the edge of my bed, unbothered that it's a rumpled mess of sheets and quilt. I don't even remember the last time I made it. And there hasn't been a guy in my room since Justin.

"If by magic you mean sewing and collecting names of places I'd like to visit before I die"—I open my closet door and rummage around on the floor for my favorite cutoffs and through the hangers for a crochet and cotton tank top that used to belong to my mom; I've always been a little afraid I'll ruin it if I wear it, but I want Noah to see it—"then yes, this is the most magical place on earth."

He removes the redheaded pin from New York City on my someday map. "Nothing wrong with having a dream, Cadie."

"Yeah? What's yours?"

"Not sure yet," he says. "I mean, I wanted to go to college but I've accomplished that, so now I have to figure out what's next. I don't know. I wouldn't mind being a park ranger."

"I've never really wanted to go to college, but I'm not going to marry my high school boyfriend, have kids before I'm even old enough to drink, and never leave High Springs, either."

"It doesn't have to be one or the other," he says, pushing the pin into the map all the way out in Montana. I wonder if there's any significance to the placement, but before I can ask, Noah speaks again. "You'll find the in-between."

Molly wanders into my room and slumps with a little

sigh to the floor at Noah's feet. It's weird seeing an animal in the house again. We had an orange-striped, mostly outdoor cat named Tangerine who went missing a couple of days after my mother's funeral. Dad speculated the cat was hit by a car, but I wonder sometimes if she missed Mom too much to stick around. And whether that's true for me, too.

Molly looks up at Noah with utter devotion, and I so understand that feeling. He catches me staring and hooks his finger around my pinkie, pulling me toward him until I'm standing between his knees. He smells good. Like soap and coffee, and as I trace the hole along the collar of his T-shirt I feel like I'm just too gross right now for this. Noah doesn't seem to mind because his arms wrap around my middle and he tumbles backward on the bed, dragging me with him. On top of him. Laughing. I kiss him and he kisses me until we're a tangle of lips and tongue, and his fingers plow shivery paths through my hair. I've never been afraid of kissing boys or afraid of saying no, but Noah makes me want to give in to the impulses swarming inside my skin like bees.

"Noah—"

"I know." He blows out a long, slow breath, and his body goes slack beneath me. "We should get moving, anyway."

"I need to take a shower." I peel myself off him and

grab my towel from the back of the desk chair. "But that was pretty magical."

Noah's face goes a little pink as he runs his hand across the top of his head, and the bashfulness is unbearably cute. "Yes, it was."

Ten minutes later, I'm clean, properly dressed for a day at O'Leno, and my hair smells like everlasting sunshine. At least that's what it says on the bottle. This time my knapsack is loaded with a change of clothes, sunscreen, a bathing suit and towel, an extra pair of underwear. I stick a return note on the fridge—with extra x's and o's on the bottom for Daniel Boone—telling Dad I'll be home tomorrow in time for work.

From my house we go to Lindsey's, and I feel thankful it looks more redneck than mine with her dad's camouflage-colored gator boat sitting on a trailer in the side yard beside an algae-green swimming pool that's probably filled with tadpoles. Then I feel guilty because after Mom died, Mrs. Buck brought us a mountain of casseroles to keep in the freezer. I feel even worse when Lindsey just jumps out of the convertible and tells us she'll be back in a few minutes, like maybe she's embarrassed, too.

"So, Cadie, is there a place we can eat alligator around here?" Matt asks. "It's one of those things I've always wanted to try."

"I heard it tastes like chicken," Noah adds.

"It kind of does," I say. "And Lindsey's dad and brothers are alligator hunting guides, so I bet they have some in their freezer right now." Without waiting for Noah to open the door for me, I climb out over the side of the car. "I'll go ask."

The Bucks never answer their front door so I go around to the back, pausing when I hear Mrs. Buck's voice through the screen. "I'm not sure I like the idea of you going off to Orlando with a couple of boys you only just met."

"They're really nice." I can barely hear Lindsey's voice, and I wonder how she's ever been heard in a house full of loud boys. She's got four brothers—three older and one younger—and all of them wilder than hogs. Ray, the one just older than us, was my first boyfriend when I was in sixth grade. I was too nervous to even kiss him so he moved on to someone who wasn't.

"I don't know, Linds."

"Cadie Wells is going, too. It'll be fine, Mama. We'll stick together."

I knock on the door to announce my presence, then go inside. They're standing in the kitchen, and Mrs. Buck catches me up in a hug like I haven't had in a long time. Her blue-and-orange UF sweatshirt smells like flour and vanilla, as if she's been baking. "Cadie, honey, how are you?"

"Real good, thanks," I say. "Busy as always."

"I bet your daddy is awful proud of you." She fusses with my hair, tucking a strand behind my ear the way my mom always did. I know it's just a motherly thing but I feel a little catch in my chest all the same. "Please tell me you won't let my girl get into any trouble."

"I won't." And the thing is, Mrs. Buck trusts me. I'm a good girl. A responsible girl. She won't even check with Dad to make sure it's okay with him—which it surely won't be. He won't be as easily fooled as she is. "I promise."

With a happy squeak, Lindsey runs off to get ready, and I ask her mother if she has any alligator to spare, which makes Mrs. Buck laugh as if I've told the funniest joke in the world. "Oh, honey, when do we ever not have gator? We've got it fresh, frozen, and dried into jerky. Pick your poison."

I go back to the car with a plastic storage bag filled with stew-size chunks of alligator meat swimming in a marinade that Mrs. Buck calls secret, but is really just soy sauce and orange juice with a shaving of ginger floating in it. A few minutes later Lindsey comes flying out of the house with an overstuffed duffel that looks as if she's packed for a week and the biggest smile I've ever seen on her face.

CHAPTER 7

CHAPTER 7

Rhea Chung is running the store when we show up for provisions: wood skewers, soy sauce, green bell peppers, sweet Vidalia onions, and cherry tomatoes for alligator kebabs, along with eggs, bacon, and beans for breakfast. Bags of ice. Beer. It's weird when Noah just opens his wallet and flashes his legal ID at Rhea since I've gotten so used to sweet-talking her into looking the other way for my friends. Instead, I ask if Dad is coming in.

"Not today." Her dark ponytail swings as she shakes her head. Her real name is Youngmi, but she told me on her first day of work that when her family immigrated to the United States, her Korean parents chose the name Rhea because they wanted to give her a real American name. I didn't tell her that it's not the most stars-and-stripes name you could have, but . . . well, my name's Arcadia so I don't have much room to talk. And in Greek mythology, Rhea was the Titan wife of Kronos, queen of heaven. It's a pretty badass name, really. "He is babysitting today so I'm working overtime."

A tiny lick of anger flares up inside me because caring for your own child is *not* babysitting and because now I feel guilty that my day off means a double shift for Rhea when it's not really my fault at all. "I'm so sorry. If you want, I can—"

"No, no, no." The ponytail swings even faster. "You work too hard, Cadie, and I can use the money. Enjoy your day off and don't worry so much."

With Rhea's blessing insulating my conscience, I follow Noah out into the sunshine. He packs the perishables with the alligator meat in a cooler in the trunk and we head up 441 to launch at the river outpost.

Noah takes the rear seat in our canoe with Molly lying in the middle, her head propped on a yellow life jacket. Along the shore, Suwannee cooter turtles are stacked like pancakes, soaking up the sunshine on rotting logs and on slivers of sandy beach, and scrub jays squawk in the oaks on both sides of the river. We paddle past the ruins of a bridge where the old road used to cross on the way to Lake City, and only about five hundred yards from the outpost we come to Columbia Spring. Decaying leaves stain the river a well-steeped-tea brown, but the spring bubbles up blue green and so clear you think you can just reach down all twenty-five feet and touch the bottom.

We don't say much as we make our way down the river, except to point out some wild turkeys, a couple of gray herons, and a six-foot alligator half-submerged near the bank. Besides, it's almost too pretty to talk. We pass the spring near the boat ramp where the water seems as if it's boiling, and the sun gets warmer as the morning reaches for midday. By Poe Spring we've cracked open bottles of water and cans of Coke.

Justin and I had only been dating about a month when we kayaked to Poe for a picnic on the dock. He wasn't old enough to drive, so his mom drove us to the outpost and signed for the rentals. And the sandwiches she packed in a little foam cooler were made of bologna salad on white bread, which I hate. I ate one anyway because we were still new and I was too polite to tell Justin's mom the truth.

I look over my shoulder at Noah, whose eyes are hidden behind black-rimmed sunglasses. "I hate bologna salad sandwiches."

"That was random." He laughs a little. "But, okay . . . I hate clam chowder."

"Seriously?" I swing all the way around to face him, letting him paddle on his own. And, I admit, I like watching the way his shoulders move as the blade cuts cleanly through the water. "How do they even let you live in Maine? I mean, you could be deported back to California for that, right?"

He puts a finger to his lips, then points to the trees. "The forest has ears."

"Well, if it makes you feel any better, I hate okra." I reach down and tickle Molly under her chin. She's such a good canoe passenger, sitting there smiling in the sun. "It's slimy and nasty and I think my status as a southerner could be revoked for saying that, but it's gross."

"Your secret's safe with me," Noah says. "I hate peanut butter and jelly."

"Shut up. Who hates PB and J?"

"I do. And tuna fish."

"God, it's like you're not even human. Stop it. Next you're going to say you like liver or red beets."

"Both, actually," he says. "But not as much as I love bologna salad."

"I want to trade canoes. Matt can't possibly be as weird as you." A wing of water from his paddle hits cold and sharp against my skin, stealing my breath. I grab for my own paddle and splash back. Then Matt joins in. And Lindsey. Before long all four of us are locked in an epic water fight—with Molly barking circles in the canoe— until we're all drenched and our shouts echo through the trees.

When we're finally settled down and I'm facing

forward again with my paddle in my hands, Noah says my name and his voice tickles up my spine, all soft and sweet, and I turn to look at him.

The corner of his mouth tilts in a bone-melting grin. "I hate bologna salad, too."

About fifteen minutes later we turn off the main river into the narrow run that leads to Lily Spring. Tacked to the trees are hand-painted signs with sayings like IF MAN WAS HALF AS SMART AS HE THINKS HE IS, HE WOULD BE TWICE AS SMART AS HE ACTUALLY IS and I WAS BORN WITH THE MOST COMFORTABLE, LEAST EXPENSIVE SWIMSUIT I'VE FOUND. Warnings that say UNATTENDED CHILDREN WILL BE USED AS ALLIGATOR BAIT. WELCOME TO LILY SPRING. And a yellow diamond-shaped caution sign that reads NAKED ED AHEAD.

"Oh my God," Matt says from the other canoe. "This is really happening."

Rounding the bend we first see a thatched palm hut that looks like it belongs on a deserted tropical island instead of in the middle of the Florida woods. Beside the spring run is a multilevel dock, and Naked Ed is standing on the highest level, wearing only a loincloth that resembles a furry brown string bikini and a tribal-looking necklace. Even his head is naked, although his chin is covered in gray fur that matches the hair on his chest and protruding belly.

When my friends and I were little, we all thought

Naked Ed was some sort of ancient hermit. We'd scare each other with stories about how if you stuck a single toe in Lily Spring he'd get you and you'd never see your family again. Now that I see him with his grandpa glasses and smiling face, I realize he's not so old. Sixty-something maybe.

"Howdy." Naked Ed waves as we beach the canoes and Noah clips a leash on Molly. "If it'll make the ladies more comfortable, I can keep the loincloth on."

Even though it should go without saying that I've seen naked guys before—most recently this very morning—I'm not too keen on seeing old Ed's dangly bits. "That would be great, thanks," I say.

He invites us to swim in the spring—nude, if we like— but after yesterday's fiasco I'm not too keen on skinny-dipping, either. Noah and Lindsey strip down to their bathing suits and wade into the spring, but Matt climbs up on the dock and I follow him. Ed gestures toward a pair of white plastic chairs in an unspoken offer to sit.

"I like your hair," he says, holding my hand an extra-long moment as we shake. His fingers are warm and not at all papery and dry like old-people fingers. "With those blue eyes you look like an upside-down sunrise."

"Wouldn't that be a sunset?" Matt says over my shoulder.

"Nope." Naked Ed doesn't elaborate, and he winks

at me as he releases my hand to greet Matt. "But it sure is pretty." Ed says "sure" like "shore" and "pretty" like "purdy," which puts me at ease because he's one of my people. To a stranger like Matt he might be a novelty, but I feel a kinship and a protectiveness I didn't expect.

"So, if you don't mind my asking . . . how did you end up out here?" I'm tuned in to Matt's voice for hints of sarcasm or meanness, but he's just being friendly. I relax into my chair and Matt takes the other.

"Well, like the sign says—" Ed aims his hand at a large sign posted on a nearby tree. It's lettered in uneven text and bears facts about the spring and himself. "I suffer from brittle bones, and after breakin' so many of 'em it got too dangerous for me to work. Back in '85 I was canoein' out there on the river and found this spring. I figured since I liked the water and I liked skinny-dipping, I'd offer to clean up the place in exchange for letting me swim. The powers 'at be said yes, so here I am."

I hitch my knees up to my chin, propping my feet on the edge of my chair. "You know, when I was little I'd go over to my friend's house for sleepovers, and if we got too giggly late at night, her mama would tell us that if we didn't settle down Naked Ed would come get us."

This makes him hoot with laughter, and then he smiles. "Local gal, huh?"

I tell him my dad owns the market in High Springs,

and he admits that he usually prefers the prices at the Winn-Dixie.

"I collect disability pay," he says by way of explanation, and I understand this. Fixed income and not a lot of it. "But I like supporting local folks so I shop at your store, too. Next time I come to town, I'll keep an eye out for that firecracker hair."

"I can't guarantee I'll recognize you with your clothes on," I say, which busts him up all over again.

"She's a pistol, this one," Naked Ed says to Matt. "You should hang on to her."

"Oh, we're not—" I begin.

"That's the plan," Matt interrupts. His eyes meet mine, and I hope I'm not blushing, because my face is warmer than from just the Florida sun. I look down at his tanned hands and strong wrists, and I feel guilty for being attracted to him. Like I'm some greedy, boy-crazy creature when in reality I've been a girl in drought and this sudden influx of attention feels like a flash flood.

I turn my face toward the water, toward Noah, who beckons me with a sly grin and the crook of a single finger. And right there is the difference. Matt is a flutter in the belly. A harmless flirtation. But Noah is the magnetic pull that unfolds me from my chair and propels me off the dock into the spring. When I surface, he's there.

"You just charm the pants off everyone, don't you?"

His voice is low so only I can hear. I can't tell if he's teasing, but I don't think he is.

"Who, Ed?" I push my wet hair back from my face. "He's not wearing pants."

"I'm not talking about Ed."

He's not teasing.

I glance over at Lindsey—I'd kind of forgotten about her—but she's floating on her back with her eyes closed, smiling. Not listening to us about to get complicated over something that doesn't need to be. Especially because after Noah and Matt bring us back from Disney World, they will drive off toward Flamingo in the Cougar and I will go back to being Drought Girl.

"Don't be like that." I link my fingers through his as we sink down in the shallows, our knees touching underwater. My own words give me a strange déjà vu feeling that spins me back to a night when I was about eight or nine. The babysitter had already tucked me into bed, but I was still awake when Mom and Dad came home late from a night out. Through my bedroom door I heard my mother say the same words, "Come on, Danny, don't be like that."

She never called him Danny in front of me. Only Dan. So I crept across the room and pressed myself against the door, listening as Dad answered back. "Beautiful girls are easier because you know you're batting in the minors."

His words were slurry but tender. "Girls like you, Marie . . . most of the time you're an ordinary girl and the reasons you love me back make sense, but sometimes you shine so bright it hurts and I worry that I'll never, ever be able to keep you."

"You're the only one," Mom said that night. "I will tell you a million times until the day I die, if I have to. You are the only one."

Their words were like a secret language I didn't understand until now. This boy in Lily Spring does not love me the way Dad loved my mom. Love to the point of being paralyzed without it. Love doesn't enter into what's happening here because we barely know each other, but Noah's still the same kind of jealous. "It's tomorrow," I say. "Do you think you might ask me to run away again?"

"Guess it all depends on whether you're running away with me or my cousin."

"Don't be like that." This time I whisper it. "Ask me."

"Will you?"

I nod. "Absolutely."

His smile is a mile wide as he reaches for me. I'm thinking he's going to kiss me, but instead he lifts me up and tosses me into the deep water of the spring. I come up laughing as Lindsey ducks underwater and tries to grab him by the ankles. But Noah is big. Solid. And when he doesn't go down, Matt cannonballs off the dock, sending a spray in Noah's face. It takes three of us to dunk him—even then I think he lets us—and for a good long while we all take turns trying to drown each other. Until Matt suggests chicken fights.

The first round starts with me on Noah's shoulders, but Matt is smaller and Lindsey's not as strong as I am, so we take them easily. Then we swap teams and I get flustered, thinking that the way Matt's hands are wrapped around my calves means something—or that it bothers Noah—and I lose my advantage. Lindsey knocks me off Matt's shoulders with embarrassing ease until I finally get over myself.

We eat lunch on the sandy embankment and, before we continue on our way down the river, pose for pictures with Naked Ed. He gives me a hug as he encourages Lindsey and me not to be strangers.

"And if things don't work out with those fellas," he calls out as we paddle away, "you know where to find me."

CHAPTER 8

Long before Mom found out she had cancer, Dad and I would come to O'Leno a couple of times a summer for campouts. Dad would drive us up after dinner when it was still light out and pitch the old musty-smelling tent that spent the rest of the year buried in the garage. The metal-on-metal sound of his hammer hitting the stakes would ring through the trees. The sound of anticipation.

When he finished the tent, he'd build a fire and tell me stories. Ghost stories that made me burrow my face into the safety of his side. Fairy tales of evil mermaids with sharp teeth who lived in the Santa Fe River sinkholes and kept alligators as pets. And, as I got older, real-life stories about his sister, Suzanne, who ran away from High Springs and didn't come back until Mom's funeral.

Suzanne, who makes me wonder if there is a wanderlust gene in the Wells DNA that passed over Dad completely. In the morning he would cook eggs and bacon in an old cast-iron skillet right on the orange-hot firewood, and I was convinced he knew how to do everything in the world.

These days it's an event if we're both at the dinner table at the same time. And I kind of wish we could rewind time. I mean, in a perfect world we'd get Mom back, too, but even if Dad and I could just be close again it would be okay. I'm thinking about this as Matt flips the alligator kebabs on a grate over the top of the fire pit, and the dripping, sizzling marinade brings me back to the campsite.

"This smells amazing," he says. "Just for making my alligator dreams come true, Linds, you get to pick the first thing we do at Disney."

"I want to ride Space Mountain. Or, no . . . wait. Maybe we could go to the Harry Potter park first, but I've always wanted to go to Epcot Center because I doubt I'll ever actually get to go to Paris. Would it be weird if I wanted to get my picture taken with Ariel?" Until now, the total sum of words I've heard her speak since we met Matt and Noah could fit on a sticky note, but the words come out of her like she's been saving them up. "I mean, I know I'm too old for Disney princesses, but—"

"Don't hurt yourself," Matt teases. "There's time to figure it out."

"She's got a point, though," I say. "There are three or four parks, so if we're only there for a day, we kind of need a plan."

"I found an app." Lindsey taps her phone screen, and as we lose her to technology, Noah frowns at the fire. I feel bad talking about Disney World when he clearly doesn't want to go.

"Lindsey and I shouldn't come." I keep my voice low so only he can hear me, my cheek against his upper arm. This is a hard admission because I want to go. Disney World isn't a big adventure, but it's at least a step away from here. "We've taken over your trip and it's not fair."

"No. I definitely want you to come." He moves his arm around me, and I want to burrow my face into his side for a whole different reason than way back when I was with my dad. "It's just that this is getting complicated when all I wanted to do was go camping."

"Maybe we can convince them to do something else."

Except Lindsey's face shines in the glow of her cell phone as she GPS-tracks "princesses" or whatever it is she's doing, and I don't have the heart to talk her out of this.

"Yeah." Noah laughs softly, as if he's read my mind. "Good luck with that."

Matt finishes cooking the gator kebabs, and we devour them almost before they're cool enough to eat. Paddling left us all hungry, tired, and a little bit sunburned, so it's not long after we're done eating that we start yawning.

"So now what?" Matt asks. "Movies? Ice cream? Bingo? Weed?"

"We don't have an ice cream shop, and the movie tonight is lame," Lindsey says, as she stacks all the dirty paper plates in a pile.

"Your theater only shows one movie?"

"Sadly." I nod. "We roll up the sidewalks pretty early around here, and the guy with the weed went to the hospital this morning, so unless you want to drive to Gainesville for something to do, we're going to have to get creative."

"Not driving," Noah says, as he gives Molly a bite of leftover alligator. "I'm perfectly content doing nothing right here."

"This is where one of you two is supposed to pull out your travel guitar so we can sing around the campfire," I say. "Dazzle us with original lyrics and covers of too-cool-for-High-Springs songs."

Noah's laugh is low and rumbly. "I don't have a guitar, and I left my trombone back in California."

Now it's my turn to laugh. "Trombone?"

"When I was in fifth grade we had to choose between

music class or orchestra," he says. "Since I was a dirty little ska kid who wanted to be in a band, I opted out of music class and learned the trombone. I quit after a year, though, because you can only play 'Red River Valley' so many times before you want to hang yourself."

"Did you end up joining a band?" Lindsey asks.

"In ninth grade." Noah makes Molly give a high five before he rewards her with another piece of gator. "We called ourselves the Trojan All-Stars—"

"That explains the T-shirt," I say.

"Yep," he says. "We recorded a three-song ska EP in one guy's basement that completely sucked, and we took it around to all the local record shops and clubs. Everyone rejected us except my friend's cousin who booked shows for this one club. Our only paying gig was as first opening band for The Slackers, but we went on so early that no one came to see us and, seven years later, we still have nearly all the T-shirts left."

"I keep telling you," Matt says. "You offer those things online as rare and vintage, there are idiots who will pay good money for those shirts."

"I want to hear the songs," I say.

Noah shakes his head, but the corner of his mouth turns up. "You really don't."

"I really do."

"I don't have them."

"Lies." I whisper the word in his ear, and the ticklish

little shrug of his shoulder makes me feel as if I've discovered fire. "I bet a million dollars they're on your phone."

He kisses me with soy-and-ginger lips as he digs into his pocket for his cell. "You win."

He was right. All three tracks sound as if they were recorded in someone's closet. The words are mostly unintelligible, and the best part is the way Noah's trombone drowns out the singer. They're awful songs.

"God, that was . . . painful," Lindsey says.

"We were better live," Noah says, and then a beat later, "but not much."

Our laughter trickles to silence, and I'm pretty sure all four of us are racking our brains to come up with something else to do when all we really want is sleep. Or maybe that's just me.

"I hate to throw a wet blanket over this wild time we're having," I say. "But I'm really tired. I think I'm going to go use the bathroom and then crash."

Lindsey stands. "I'll come with you."

The campground is pretty quiet as we head down the loop road. A bit of music here. People sitting around fires there. I haven't been alone with Lindsey in years, and I don't know what to say to her. I fall back on something the announcer said at graduation when she walked across the stage to get her diploma. "So I didn't know you wanted to be a nurse."

Of course, the last time Lindsey and I talked about

what we wanted to be when we grow up, she was going to be a famous ballerina and I wanted to be the girl on *MythBusters*. Mostly because I liked her hair. Even then I clearly had no plan for my life.

"I started thinking about it after your mom died," Lindsey says.

"Really?"

"It's not like I could have saved her or anything just by being a nurse," she says. "But I liked the idea of being there for people, you know? Doing what you can, even if it's not fixing them."

Lindsey has always been a tender heart. She is a shoulder offerer. A giver of hugs. I've seen her bring cookies to school for her friends' birthdays. Being a nurse makes sense.

"My mom would love that," I say.

"I miss her," she says. "I remember the first time I came over to your house I thought she was a fairy because of her hair and because she wore dresses on days other than Sunday."

"See, I always liked going to your house because your mom smells like bread and gives the best hugs."

Lindsey laughs. "She does give the best hugs, doesn't she?"

"Why did we stop hanging out?"

"I don't know."

"Seems like we just drifted, and neither of us did any-thing to stop it," I say. "But the thing is, if someone asked me if I was friends with Lindsey Buck, I would say yes."

"Me, too."

The conversation ends when we reach the bathroom, and I don't want to talk while we're in the stalls because that's just plain weird, but I don't think there's anything left that needs saying. Maybe knowing we're still some kind of friends is enough.

By the time we get back to the campsite all evidence of dinner has been cleared away. Matt is emptying the melt-water from the cooler, and Noah has Molly by the leash.

"We're going for a walk," he tells me. "Come with?"

"Would you mind if I didn't?"

"Nope," he says. "I won't be long."

"I'll come." Lindsey hangs a washcloth on the clothes-line, and the three of them head away from the campsite, Noah's flashlight beam cutting through the darkness.

"Excited for tomorrow?" Matt lowers himself beside me on the big log. Not too close, but enough that I can feel his warmth fill the space that separates us.

"If it wasn't for Lindsey, I wouldn't care if we went to Disney World at all," I say. "But I think we're going to have a good time."

"What would you rather do?"

"I don't know," I say. "I guess—today was really fun."

Matt nods. "Naked Ed seemed to like you."

"It's a local thing."

"No it's not," he says. "You're just really—"

"After you guys bring us back," I interrupt, not wanting to hear that I am really anything, "if you want weird stuff, you should check out the Devil's Chair down in Cassadaga. The rumor goes that the devil will appear to anyone bold enough to sit in the chair at midnight. And that if you leave an unopened can of beer on the chair, the beer will be gone by morning. Some people claim the can will still be unopened, but—"

Matt closes the gap and presses his lips against mine. I pull back, but not fast enough and not before my brain registers soft. Warm. Nice.

"We should, um—" I stand quickly. "We should probably leave here early tomorrow. So, I'm going to turn in now."

"Cadie, wait."

I don't wait because who is this strange girl who lets two guys kiss her on the same day? I mean, I believe a girl can kiss as many guys as she damn well pleases and not have to feel bad about it. She can even do more than kiss someone if she wants. I'm just not sure I'm brave enough to be that girl. Because right now my stomach is a pit of eels, and I can't even meet Matt's eye. "Good night."

"Cadie," he calls after me, as I hurry toward Noah's tent. "I didn't mean to do that. I'm sorry."

Zipped safely inside, I change into the old white under-shirt and school gym shorts combo I usually wear for sleeping. I mean to wait up for Noah, and for a while I'm successful as my brain plays Matt's kiss on repeat. I fret over whether or not I invited it. Whether or not I wanted it. But my shoulders ache from paddling, and eventually I feel myself drifting off.

I have no idea what time it is when the air mattress shifts under Noah's weight and he wraps himself around me the way he did last night. We fall asleep, and I don't wake again until the morning sun makes the tent seem as if aglow from the inside—and my phone vibrates with an incoming text message.

I had to go home. Sorry. −L

At first my sleep-fogged brain can't decipher the message because I can't think of anyone I know whose name begins with *L*. Then I realize it's Lindsey, but that doesn't make any sense, either, because we're going to Disney World so there's no way she would leave. My phone flashes a reminder that I need to charge the battery as I text a message back to her.

Everything okay?

A minute passes. Then two. Noah shifts, and Molly shakes, her collar jingling before she gets to her feet and nudges her nose into my hand. But I get no answer from Lindsey.

"Noah." I say his name softly so I won't scare him

awake, but his eyes pop open immediately and they have that slightly wild look. "Sorry. It's just— Lindsey left."

"She left?"

I show him the text screen on my phone.

"Weird." He sits up, rubs the back of his head, disrupting the sunbeams that hang in the air behind him, and yawns. "She was really stoked about Disney. It's all she could talk about last night when we walked the dog."

"I hope it wasn't an emergency."

"My guess is that it wasn't," Noah says. "I mean, she would have woken us up for an emergency, right? And I could have driven her anywhere she needed to go quicker than waiting for a ride to come. Maybe she changed her mind and was too embarrassed to admit it."

I unzip the tent and step out with bare feet. The ground is warm, and Matt is cracking eggs into a cast-iron skillet just the way my dad used to do it. Matt's even toasting the bread over the fire, which makes it feel like he's been digging around inside my head. He smiles at me as if last night's kiss never happened. " 'Morning. Coffee is on the table, and breakfast should be ready in a minute or so."

"Lindsey left."

"What? Seriously?" His eyebrows register confusion as he turns over the toast to get the top as golden brown as the bottom. "I just assumed she was already up, taking a shower or something. Why did she leave?"

"I don't know." I tell Matt about her text and share Noah's theory.

"Yeah, maybe." Matt transfers the eggs and toast onto a plate and carries them over to the picnic table. "Or maybe she was worried about money."

Truth be told, I'm a little worried about the money myself, so he definitely makes a good point.

Noah comes out of the tent with Molly following, her leash dragging on the ground behind her. The state park has regulations about dogs being on leashes, but Molly rarely ventures far away from Noah. I mean, who can blame her? I've only known him a little more than a day, and I want to follow him everywhere.

"Now that Lindsey's bailed, what are you going to do?" he asks. "Do you still want to come with us?"

My dad will be annoyed if I tell him I'm not coming home today. And I worry about who will take care of Danny, because even if I'm not his mother, he's still my little boy. I feel selfish, but I nod anyway. "Just let me make some calls."

My phone complains at me again about my battery, so I text Dad that I'm taking another day off. It's the coward's way out—and one more reason I can see why Lindsey may have left without telling us in person—but I don't want to fight with my dad. Being a coward suits me just fine.

Then I message Duane to ask if he and Jess would

mind helping out with my brother today. It's early so I don't expect it when Duane calls me back right away. "Where ya going, Cadie?"

"The Devil's Chair." I am changing the plan because Noah doesn't want to go to Disney. "It's in—"

"Cassadaga, I know. Me and the Kendricks and some people went looking for it last year," he says, and it hits me that I wasn't invited on that road trip. I expected to be left out of stuff by my ex-boyfriend, but not my best friend. That kind of stings. "Who are you going with?" Duane asks.

"Two guys from Maine I met at the campfire party. The ones with the '69 Cougar."

"Do you know how crazy that sounds?" he asks. "Cadie that I know doesn't go road-tripping with strangers."

"Cadie that you know doesn't do much of anything," I say. "Please, Duane? I don't know how much more I can take before I actually will go crazy. Just—when was the last time I did anything like this?"

He's quiet for a couple of beats. "Never, I guess."

"Then have a little faith, okay?"

"How long you fixin' to be gone?"

"Late tonight, maybe, or early tomorrow?" My words are a question as I look at Noah and he nods.

"Jess is off today, so she can go pick up the rug rat." Duane sighs, and inside it I hear everything he's not saying.

"I know this is asking a lot—" I say.

"Just be careful, Cadie. And if you get in a jam—I mean anything at all—you call me right away. Got it?"

"Yep."

"Have fun, crazy girl."

"Thanks, Duane. Love you."

He tells me to shut up, and then he's gone. It's just me and Noah and Matt, and they're both looking at me.

"We're not going to Disney World," I say.

A matched set of grins is what I get in return as I shovel a fork filled with yolky toast into my mouth, but it's Matt who speaks first. "So what's next? Devil's Chair?"

I nod. "Let's go hear what the devil has to say."

CHAPTER 9

CHAPTER 9

Mom used to keep a little box of cards printed with questions and quotes. Conversation starters, she'd call them, and she'd take them out at the dinner table whenever I was having a one-word-answer day or if Dad carried on too long with work-related gripes. It wasn't as much a family bonding exercise as it was a way for her to force us to talk to her about something after she'd spent most of her day alone. Usually I didn't mind, even the times I rolled my eyes. But when she was pregnant and riddled with cancer, she was the one who didn't want to talk sometimes. Dad and I never pulled out the box for her, and after she was gone . . . well, I don't even know where the cards are. We don't talk like that anymore, my dad and me. More often than not our conversations are night ships.

Did you do your homework?
Yeah.
There's a plate in the oven for you.
Thanks.
The grass is looking long.
I'll mow it after school.

I appreciate that my dad's life sucks sometimes, too. There are nights I lean against the wall outside his door, wanting to knock. Touching the pencil mark on the frame from the last time he measured me there. Wanting him to invite me in. Pressing my ear against the wood grain as if I might hear his thoughts. Wanting to share in the bit of Mom that's still left in that room. But I'm afraid I'll break him more than he's already been broken.

All of this is why, when I finally hear from Dad, I'm not surprised that his reply is a text message telling me I've had my fun, but now it's time to come home, preferably in time to make dinner. Keeping the confrontation as short and impersonal as possible. Like father, like daughter. Only we're halfway to Cassadaga and I'm not asking Noah to turn the car around now.

I'm typing a response when I'm interrupted by an incoming text from Lindsey.

Everything's okay. Just a family thing I forgot about.

Before I can find out what was more important to her than Disney World, my phone powers off. Dead.

Perfect.

I lean forward between the seats to tell Noah and Matt about Lindsey's response.

"Bummer," Matt says, but he doesn't sound especially upset. Noah doesn't say anything and I wonder if Lindsey even matters to them. If I matter. Maybe I'm just another Florida tourist attraction. Then again, how could I be anything more?

"My phone died," I say. "Do either of you have a charger?"

But they have expensive, gadgety phones that talk to them and play hours of music. Not compatible with my old model that only makes calls and texts. I'm not complaining about it. Just that of all the things I remembered to bring, my charger wasn't one of them.

"Do you need to make a call?" Noah offers me his phone, but I decide I'll wait until we reach Cassadaga. A few more miles isn't going to keep my dad from being upset when I tell him I'm not coming home.

The backseat of the Cougar is comfortable, but the one thing I've learned about convertibles since we left High Springs is that at sixty miles per hour they aren't as romantic as they seem. I've peeled the same strand of hair out of my mouth about 642 times, the music just *wah-wah-wahs* from the speakers, and unless we're shouting, talking isn't all that easy. Of course, in the grand scheme of problems, these are not bad ones to have—and it gets infinitely better after we stop outside Ocala for gas and a bathroom break for the dog. Noah tosses the keys to Matt and hops over the side of the car into the backseat with me and Molly.

"Hey!" Matt protests. "Am I the chauffeur now?"

"You wanted to drive Miss Kitty." Noah stretches his arms out along the top of the seat, tilting his face to soak up the sun. I feel his fingertips tapping out a rhythm on my shoulder, and I'd swear to it that my heart starts beating in time. "And I want to sit back here with Cadie. I'd call that a win for everybody."

Matt's hand reaches between the front bucket seats, his middle finger extended, but his reflection in the rearview mirror is laughing as he pulls the Cougar back out onto Route 40.

"Miss Kitty?" I slide up against Noah so I can talk without my words getting blown away. "Is that really the name of your car?"

"Yep," he says. "She belonged to our granddad, but she's been garaged ever since he died. Grandmother Mac-Neal would probably be rolling over in her grave if she knew we had it out on the road."

"Were you close to her?"

"Not even a little bit." He smiles to himself and shakes his head. "The first time I met her I had a foot-high, bright-red Mohawk. She looked me up and down, wrinkled her nose like she was smelling something bad, and told me I looked just like my father. So I did the same thing. Looked her up and down, wrinkled my nose, and said, 'He is quite a handsome son of a bitch, isn't he?'"

I clap my hand over my mouth to keep from laughing, but I laugh anyway. "And she still willed Miss Kitty to you?"

"Maybe in the end she was proud of me for getting myself straight and going to college," he says. "Maybe she felt bad because Matt's family inherited everything else, which makes sense because my dad can't be trusted with money or nice things. Or maybe she liked that I didn't take her shit. I don't know, but I do know I love this car."

"It's pretty hot."

Noah leans down close so his lips brush against my earlobe, and my insides feel as if someone has set off a string of firecrackers. "I haven't made out with anyone in the backseat yet. Wanna break it in?"

I can't keep from smiling. "Might be fun."

"I guarantee it." Noah's hand comes up and curls softly around the back of my neck as his mouth touches mine. No one has ever kissed me the way he does. Intense, but not hard. Sweet, but not soft. Like if he drew his lips away right now a piece of my soul might just follow along behind. Which sounds completely insane in a head with a history of being level, but I can't help thinking it. And wanting more, even if I'm just a tourist attraction.

"I'm still in the car, you guys! I can see you!" Matt shouts, his words wedging themselves between Noah and me, pulling us apart. "Have pity on the guy whose date abandoned him, would ya?"

Noah rolls his eyes, but the two of them grin at each other in the rearview mirror.

I shift positions, lying on the back bench-style seat with my feet propped on the door frame, my head on his thigh. "Do you mind?"

"Do I mind your head on my thigh?"

"No, I meant feet on the door," I say. "If it's a problem . . ."

"I never gave a shit what Grandma thought when she was alive, so you"—Noah leans down and kisses me again, quick, like we're doing it in secret—"can put your feet anywhere you want."

My imaginary road trip had us holding hands and kissing at stoplights, but in reality, Molly and I both fall asleep against Noah and I don't wake until his voice burrows its way into my brain. "Cadie, we're here."

My eyes open and his face hovers above mine, and I smile because I'm pretty sure I could get used to looking at that face. "Hi, you."

"Hey," he says, as I sit up and finger-comb through the

snarls in my windblown hair. My face is warm from the sun, and my nose stings a little, making me wonder if it's burned.

"So what do we do until midnight?" Matt asks, as we pass the welcome post for the Southern Cassadaga Spiritualist Camp. Established in 1894 by a medium who was led to the area by three ghosts after being told during a séance he would found his own spiritualist community. The whole thing sounds hokey to me, but the street is lined with new age shops—with names like Purple Rose and Sixth Sense—offering gemstones, spiritualist books, and psychic readings. Clearly there are many here who believe.

Tarot. Palm. Crystals. Astrology. Some of the mediums even claim to be able to contact loved ones on the other side. The thought of being able to talk to my mom again cuts a keen sadness through my heart.

"We could take a ghost tour or go to a psychic." I don't really believe I could communicate with my mother through a medium, but having my palm read or my tarot done might be fun. I've never done anything like that before, except the time Hallie Kernaghan brought an old Ouija board to soccer camp and a bunch of us tried to make it do something. We spent half the night accusing each other of pushing the pointer and just gave up. "Maybe a psychic can tell us who tied Jason to a tree," I say. "Or maybe she can channel your grandma's spirit so we can ask her how she feels about you driving the car."

"Oh, I'm sure she'll tell us tonight at the Devil's Chair," Matt says. "I mean, imagine it. The stroke of midnight, when the veil between worlds is thin enough for the devil to send a message. It's dark and silent in the cemetery until a disembodied voice from the deepest pits of hell shrieks, 'That car was in mint condition!'"

Noah laughs so hard that tears trickle from the corners of his eyes, and every time he tries to speak, his words get lost in a new fit of laughter. In the end we agree to grab lunch, pitch the tents at a local park, and then come back for a psychic reading—and maybe even a ghost tour—before we try out the Devil's Chair. But the first thing on my personal to-do list is call home, and it's no exaggeration when I say I'd rather speak to the devil himself than tell Dad I'm not coming home yet. I borrow Noah's phone.

"Where the hell are you?" My dad is so mad his words surely must have rattled the satellites on their way to my ear. The last time he was this upset with me was when I stole Mom's favorite perfume to wear on a date with Justin. She always let me borrow it when she was alive, but afterward Dad hoarded the bottle in his magpie nest of memories, hidden away behind his bedroom door.

He caught me red-handed and shouted at me, telling

me I had no business going in his room. That I had no
right to touch Mom's belongings, as if she'd been only his.
I tried to explain that if she were still alive she would give
me permission to use her perfume, but he just wouldn't
listen. Finally, I hurled the bottle at the living room wall
and it shattered, raining glass onto the carpet and releas-
ing Mom's scent in the house, where it hung like a ghost
for days. We didn't speak to each other until it was gone,
and even then neither of us apologized.

"Cassadaga," I tell him now. "I'll be home soo—"

"Now. You come home right now."

"No." The word lashes out of my mouth like a slap.
Hard. Fast. And other words—terrible words—bubble up
behind that word, but I swallow them in front of Noah
and Matt. "Not yet."

"This is not something you get to decide, Arcadia,"
Dad says.

"Yeah, actually it is."

"What?"

"I'm eighteen years old." I cringe as I say it, because
playing the legal-adult card doesn't make me feel like an
adult at all. It makes me feel like a brat, but I say it anyway. "So I *do* get to decide."

"My house, my rules."

"Dad—"

"Cadie, you are still my daughter and—"

"Exactly," I say. "I'm your daughter. Danny is your son. You're supposed to take care of us, but all I've done for the last three years is take care of you. I just want this one thing. Just—"

"Be back in time for dinner," he says, softer now, but still firm. Disappointment washes through me. I thought—I hoped—he'd relent. "And bring Lindsey Buck with you."

"Wait, what? Dad?"

He hangs up before I can tell him Lindsey already went home, and I'm left with nothing but an earful of dial tone. Why would he say that? Why doesn't he know that she didn't come with us? And if she's not at home . . . where is she?

"That's weird." I hand Noah his phone. "He seems to think Lindsey is with us."

"Where else would she go?" he asks.

"I don't know."

"Do you want to call her?" He extends the phone to me again and I take it, except Lindsey assured me she was okay. And her business hasn't been my business in a long time. Still, I told her mom I'd look out for her. I open the keypad, and, after all that wrangling with my conscience, it hits me that I don't even know Lindsey's cell number by heart. I try their old landline, which I think the Bucks abandoned in favor of a cellular family plan, and get recorded confirmation that I have no way of contacting Lindsey. I could call Dad again, but . . . no thanks.

Matt jingles the keys to the Cougar. "Do you want us to take you back?"

"No." The more my dad wants me to come home, the less I am inclined. He doesn't want his daughter, he wants the cook, the housekeeper, and the babysitter.

"You sure?" Noah asks.

Molly nuzzles her nose under my hand so I'll pet her and I do. "Trying to get rid of me?"

He shakes his head and makes an I-can't-believe-you're-really-asking-me-that-question face. "Nope."

"Well—" I miss my little brother something fierce. I don't think we've been apart this many days before, but isn't that part of the problem? Even though I can justify what I'm doing, it doesn't keep me from feeling guilty. I'm just getting better at tamping it down. When I smile at Noah I mean it. I don't want to leave. "I guess I'm staying."

The lady across the table from me doesn't look psychic. Granted, my only frame of reference is Esmeralda, the grandma fortune-teller inside the machine at the antique shop next door to our grocery store. The machine doesn't work anymore, but my dad gave me the printed card that dropped out for him back when he was a kid. It has a four-leaf clover printed on it, a kind of get-out-of-jail-free card for when you need a little extra luck. I keep it in my wallet, but I'm not completely convinced good luck is transferrable like that.

Anyway, the lady across the table from me looks like someone's mom and the school photos of moon-faced kids hanging on the living room wall behind her suggest she may well be. So incongruous with the purple neon hand in her living room window offering palm, tarot, aura, and astrological readings for twenty dollars.

She tells me her name is Joan, which seems pretty unexotic, but see: Esmeralda. Beggars can't be choosers, and the good-luck card in my wallet doesn't have much company—only the fifty-dollar bill Uncle Eddie gave me for graduation, ten dollars Justin's mom slipped me at the football stadium after the ceremony, and a fifteen-dollar Target gift card from Rhea Chung. I should probably save the money for something important, but when in Cassadaga, I guess. So here we are.

Joan distributes her tarot cards on the table in a row of six—a universal spread, she calls it—and flips over the first one. On it is a woman wearing a white dress, with an apple in one hand and some sort of branch in the other. It's very beautifully illustrated, and I remind myself to ask her the name of the deck.

"This card represents how you feel about yourself right

now." Joan touches it with a manicured hand. So pretty compared to my ragged nails. "The High Priestess means you are seeking guidance and answers. Your life is out of balance, and you're looking for guidance but need to look within yourself. You need to trust your intuition."

Generic, but nice, and the part about my life being out of balance is pretty accurate.

The second card is the Fool.

"This doesn't mean you're a fool," Joan assures me. "It usually means you just want to be happy and that you're trying to find the thing that will bring that happiness. You feel unsure of what you want in life, and you're ready for new experiences, personal growth, and maybe even adventure. That's why it's important to remember the High Priestess, who tells you to trust your instincts."

My brain pricks up like dog ears at the word "adventure," but I don't say anything. Again, she is not wrong, but the card meaning is vague enough that it could be applied to anyone.

I nod.

"I get a sense with you that you have great musical ability," she says. "Do you sing?"

"In the shower," I say. "And not very well."

"Maybe the piano or—no, guitar." Gathering dust in the corner of my closet is an old guitar that used to belong to my dad. He gave it to me because at thirteen—after my

MythBusters phase—I was going to be a rock star. Turns out I was hopelessly bad at playing guitar. I shake my head. "Well, it's a little hazy, and I could be seeing artistic, rather than music. But cultivate it. Nurture it. Because it will pay off in a big way."

Right.

"The Fool also might mean you're having mixed feelings about someone and whether or not you want to begin a relationship with him," she says.

I don't respond to that, either, because Matt and Noah are sitting on a bench on her front porch. She can see the backs of their heads through the window, so I'm not convinced this card isn't a gimme, too.

"Here the future is a little more clear," she says. "His name starts with an *N*. Maybe Nathan. Noah. Nicholas. I'm not sure, but either you know him or you've known him in a past life."

Did I say Noah's name while I was waiting for my turn? Could she have heard me speaking to him as I paged through a photo album filled with testimonials from happy customers? I don't think I did, but I still don't fully believe. Especially because throwing in the part about my past life kind of covers Joan's ass. I wonder if this is why her readings are so cheap.

She doesn't say any more about my love life. Instead she turns over the next card, which bears an emperor holding the world in his hand and what looks like a sheaf of arrows. A golden bird—a hawk, maybe, or a falcon—rests on his shoulder.

"The Emperor," she says. "This card means you're feeling as if success is just out of your grasp and that you don't have the support that you need—I think from your father. Perhaps a boy—no, definitely your father."

There's no way she could know that I'm torn between the desire to leave High Springs and the fear of leaving my dad and Danny behind. That I'm afraid to tell Dad that trying to fill my mom's shoes is too much for me to bear.

But Joan knows.

I stare at the Emperor, not wanting to meet her eyes as she taps his golden crown. "Trust your dad, Cadie," she says. "There's something blocking the two of you. Something to do with your mother, I think, so you'll have to make the first move. Ask him. Talk to him."

And suddenly, what started out as woolly has taken a turn toward the believable, and I'm not sure what to think. I watch as she turns over the fourth card—a castle turret on a small rocky island with Neptune (or maybe Poseidon) in the foreground, zapping the turret with his trident. A piece of turret has broken away, poised to fall into the raging ocean.

"The Tower suggests that a big change is coming," Joan says. "It will be difficult and painful, but when you come out on the other side, you will be stronger and better for it."

"What does that mean?"

"I'm not sure," she says. "The air around you feels heavy, like just before a big storm, and I can't pinpoint if the change is emotional or physical, but I do get a very strong sense that your foundation will be shaken. You must go through it. You can't go backward. You can't go home."

I'm barely breathing and my eyes are fixed on her fingers, on the cards, and we both know I've stepped across the border into the realm of belief. There are only two cards left, and I want to know what this universal spread has in store for me.

The next card depicts a man in a white tunic with a red toga. At his feet are a cup and a sword and some other things I can't identify, but right now I'm more interested in what it means.

"Typically," Joan says, "the Magician is a good sign. It means that you have all the tools to get what you want—provided you know what you want—but I'm troubled by this position in the spread."

"Why?"

"Here, the Magician represents the forces working against you," Joan says. "And I get the sense that someone—a man, a boy, definitely male—isn't quite what he seems. He is deception and trickery disguised as charm and friendliness, and he may not have your best interests at heart." She returns her hand to the High Priestess. "Trust your instincts where he is concerned."

Noah comes to mind, and I suffer a private bout of shame for even thinking of him like that. He told me about the fight that got him sent to Maine, even when he didn't want to talk about it. I've met his dog. I've seen his library cards. He's not deception and trickery, he's just an ordinary guy with a bumpy history, so I file those doubts away in the same skeptical place I did her predictions about my musical abilities. I trust my inner High Priestess. "What's next?"

She reveals the final card—a man wrestling a lion.

"Strength," Joan says. "This is the outcome card. You need to have courage, to believe in yourself, in order to get what you want. Believe in yourself and look inside when you feel your courage failing and you will succeed."

It feels as if we've doubled back to generic, and now I find myself unsure of whether what I've just experienced is real or ridiculous. I stand. She stands. I'm about to thank her for her time when Joan takes my hand as if to shake it.

"I know you're skeptical, but—" A sharp breath steals her words away and her eyes go closed behind her glasses for a beat. Then two. When they open, they're wide blue and startled. She blinks at me. "Oh." She blinks again. "Oh my." Joan pulls her hand back, rubbing her thumb against her first two fingers as if she's been shocked.

"What just happened?" The hair on the back of my neck prickles, even though I didn't feel anything other than the touch of her fingers on my hand.

"I'm not sure." Her voice is barely a whisper and she sounds as confused as I am. In a tiny corner of my heart, I hope it's my mom, somehow, here with us. Sending a message.

"Sometimes, once in a while, I'll get a flash," Joan says. "A vision. Whether it's a memory or a premonition, I'm never sure, but when I touched your hand just now I saw a tattoo. A flaming Sacred Heart tattoo. I also saw a gun, Cadie. A handgun. Do you know someone with a tattoo like that? Does this mean anything to you?"

Noah comes to mind again, but I've seen his tattoos. He doesn't have a Sacred Heart. He doesn't have a heart at all.

He doesn't have a heart at all?

Why would I think that, using those particular words? I'm unsettled and shaky, and I don't like that I'm reading so much—too much—into this when it was just supposed to be fun.

"No." I shake my head as I back away, toward the door. "But thanks. I should, um—thank you."

"It's a message, Cadie, a warning," Joan says, as I reach

for the handle of the front door, and her words reel me back. A message? "Don't give him your heart. He will break you."

"Who?" I turn to look at her, but Joan shakes her head. "I don't know."

This vision of my future, this warning, is frightening. I don't want this. I want ridiculous predictions of fame by way of the guitar I haven't touched in years. I want to go back to being skeptical because this reality is that I should be afraid because he—whoever he is—doesn't just want to break my heart, he wants to break *me*.

"So, how'd it go?" Matt scoots over to make room between him and Noah on the bench out front, but I don't sit. I pace, trying to untangle the knots my insides have become. "Are you going to be famous? Marry a man named Matt MacNeal? Please tell me she gave you the winning Super Lotto numbers."

"You okay?" The sweet note of Noah's concern bumps up against the psychic's warning, and I can't look at him when I don't know how I'm supposed to feel. She told me to trust my instincts and then said someone is going to break me. Someone with a tattoo and a gun. "Cadie, you look freaked out. What the hell happened in there?"

"She touched my hand and saw something . . ." Giving voice to the words makes me feel silly, especially since there's a line of worry in the space between Noah's furrowed brows, and Matt's usually sunny smile slides off his face. I sit down on the bench between them. "I guess like a premonition or something. I don't know. It's stupid."

"What did she see?" Matt asks.

Now that I'm out in the cool shade with the breeze kissing my skin, the whole encounter seems melodramatic and unreal. The unsettled feeling begins to break loose, and the further I get from Joan's words, the less meaning they hold. Telling them would just be embarrassing.

"She said I was going to marry Jason Kendrick, which would freak anyone out." As I fake-laugh, Noah looks at me as if he knows I'm lying, but doesn't call me out on it. I stretch my arms around both their shoulders. "So what's next? Are you guys going to have your futures read?"

"Nah." Noah shakes his head. "I don't believe in letting the lines on my hand or a deck of cards dictate how I live my life."

"Exactly," Matt agrees. "We make our own futures. And mine . . . is going to be outstanding."

CHAPTER 10

We're aimlessly meandering the back roads around Cassadaga, wasting gas and killing time until midnight, when we come across the Our Lady of the Lakes Summer Festival. Carnival music and the shrieks of those brave enough to try the carny rides stretch out to the highway. The colored lights of the skeletal-looking rides are muted in the daylight, but they're still a siren's song for three people in need of something to do.

"We should go." Matt, reading my mind, pokes his face between the front seats. "Elephant ears. Tilt-a-Whirl. Corn dogs. Dude, look"—he taps Noah's shoulder and points in the direction of a giant steel wheel—"Ring of Fire."

Noah does a vigorous head-bob, a smile breaking across his face. "We should go."

Parked cars spill out of the regular church lot into an adjoining dirt field. Clearly a popular festival. Noah finds a space at the back in the shade of some trees. Perfect for Molly, dozing on the backseat floor after an hour of non-stop fetch back at our campsite in the park. How Noah's not suffering a sore arm after all that throwing is beyond me. We leave the dog a bowl of bottled water—he says she'll be okay—and buy our admissions to the carnival.

"You guys are really planning to go on the rides?" I ask, as a man stamps the back of my hand with glow-in-the-dark ink. "I mean, why would you trust anything that collapses to fit in a truck? They're like portable death traps."

"Exactly what makes them so much fun," Matt says. "And you haven't really lived until you've experienced Ring of Fire."

"On the other hand, I haven't really died, either."

Noah laughs. "We've both ridden it and lived to tell the tale."

"Now it's your turn," Matt says.

The rides midway is at the opposite end of a gauntlet of food stands that taunt us with the scent of Italian sausage, deep-fried foods, and a sweet note of powdered sugar that reminds me of my mom.

Every spring, usually in April, High Springs holds Pioneer Days. There's a midway of homemade food and crafts tents, pony rides, a Wild West–style shootout between cowboy reenactors, an old-timey tractor show, and historical Native American displays. It's not fancy and might be considered slightly cheesy, but most everyone in High Springs turns out and it's just small-town nice.

When I was about six—right around the time I developed an obsession for the Little House on the Prairie books—Mom sewed me a blue calico dress and matching sunbonnet that I wore to Pioneer Days. Jason Kendrick was chasing me through the park on Saturday afternoon when I fell and tore a hole in the dress. After she wiped my tears and convinced me a calico patch would be even more Laura Ingalls than the original, Mom introduced me to funnel cakes. Eventually I outgrew the dress and moved past the Little House books, but every year my mom and I would share a funnel cake at Pioneer Days.

"Would you do it for some cotton candy? Fried pickles?" Noah asks.

"Seriously?" I give him a side-eye, but I'm smiling. "You think you can bribe me with food?"

"Yep."

"Funnel cake," I say. "Or we have no deal."

"Funnel cake, it is."

Ring of Fire, as it turns out, has a roller coaster train attached to a track on the inside of the giant steel wheel.

As the track spins with a metallic rattling roar, it sends the train upside down at the top of the ring. I've been on upside-down rides before at Busch Gardens over in Tampa, but as the three of us buckle into our seats, I'm a little nervous. Riders were screaming as we waited in line—some in terror, some with delight—and the top of the train is enclosed in a protective steel cage that is anything but reassuring.

The ride starts out with the train swinging forward and backward as it gains momentum—each time climbing a little higher up the ring until we're nearly upside down. I can see people walking the midway. Hear game callers attempting to lure festival goers into trying their hands at balloon darts and ring toss. But as the train moves faster, I lose sight of the midway. My hair goes crazy in the wind. We loop forward. Loop backward. I hear someone screaming—and I think it might be me—and across from me Noah and Matt are laughing.

"Well?" Matt asks, as the train swings back to a stop at the end of the ride. "What do you think?"

"It was terrifying and awesome," I say. "I think I'm a carny ride convert."

"I knew it." He and Noah high-five as if they didn't expect any other answer. "More?"

"Yes."

We ride a crazy contraption more terrifying than Ring

of Fire called the Zipper. It's a fast, oblong Ferris wheel with cage cars that rotate a three-sixty all by themselves. With every spin I feel as if I'm going to fall out, but have no idea which way I'm facing. We hit up the Tilt-a-Whirl, the Himalaya, and a bunch of other spinning rides. Noah makes good on our funnel cake deal and we eat corn dogs, too, arguing ketchup versus mustard (ketchup). We ride the swinging pirate ship that looks tame but threatens a corn dog reappearance, and then make our way to the games midway.

After I lose a buck trying to pop balloons with darts and waste another dollar at the ring-the-bottle booth, we stop at the rabbit-shooting gallery. The back wall of the booth is lined with cubbies filled with plush animals ranging from palm-size frogs to giant clown fish that look just like Nemo. A sign along the front promises THE MORE YOU HIT, THE BIGGER THE PRIZE. The target is a row of seven metal rabbits. Knock down four rabbits and you get an unnaturally green frog. Five wins a penguin wearing a purple scarf. The prize for six rabbits is a brown plush owl with a floral-print belly. And seven downed rabbits wins the fish.

"God, my brother would lose his mind over that Nemo."

I give the game operator a five-dollar bill and pick up one of the BB rifles chained to the front of the booth. I've handled a BB gun before. Just about every boy I know owns one, and in middle school we'd have shooting contests in the Kendricks' backyard, trying to hit soda cans off their back fence. Once, the boys started shooting at one another and Duane took a round shot to his backside. He was too embarrassed to go to the hospital, so my uncle Eddie removed the BB with a paring knife and tweezers.

I'm not a very good shot. I hit four out of the seven, and the game operator gives me one of the frogs. It has a pink ribbon tied around the neck. It's cute.

"Let me try." Noah offers up his own five-dollar bill and chooses one of the BB guns from the end of the counter.

Matt adds another fiver. "I'll try, too."

They're very serious about the game, each positioning himself at the counter, one eye lined up along the top of the rifle and the other eye squinted shut. They squeeze off their first shots very slowly and deliberately. *Plink. Plink.* Two rabbits down. A little crowd gathers behind us to watch.

Another *plink, plink.* Another two rabbits down.

Matt and Noah shoot neck-and-neck through three, four, five, six. Down to the last rabbit. Noah takes his final shot first.

He misses.

The game operator gives him one of the medium-size owls. It reminds me of the owls on Mom's old apron, and I immediately love it. Noah offers it to me with an apology in his eyes, as if winning a giant fish is actually important.

"I can try again," he says, but even as the words are coming out of his mouth, Matt hits his seventh rabbit with one last *plink*. A small cheer goes up behind him. A bit of clapping.

"I'll take the fish," Matt says. The game operator hands over the prize, and Matt presents it to me with a flourish and a bow. "For Daniel Boone."

The plush Nemo is not quite as big as my brother, but I can picture the thing taking up half his toddler bed, because he's definitely going to want to sleep with it.

"He's going to love this so much," I say. "Thank you."

I want to tell Noah I love the owl, too. That I'm going to keep it for myself as a souvenir of today. Of him. But his expression has morphed from apologetic to annoyed, and maybe a little jealous that Matt made the winning shot. A thank-you from me now would feel tacked on. Too late. Instead I catch his hand in mine. "Come ride the Ferris wheel with me?"

"Don't you mean you, Matt, and the big-ass fish?"

"No." My fingertips touch the back of his neck, and I gently pull his face toward mine. My lips against his are a whisper. A hint. A promise. "Just me."

Leaving Matt to look after the big-ass fish, we walk toward the rides midway, where the colored lights on the Ferris wheel are just starting to come alive in the fading day. The sun hasn't set yet, but if we're lucky, we'll catch it at the top.

We are at the top when the sun sets, but we miss it completely.

The growl of the Cougar's engine seems alive and predatory in the stillness that follows us from our campsite to the cemetery on the outskirts of town. Tonight feels so much darker than last, and the world is buzzy around the edges from the beers we drank in the cemetery parking lot while we waited for midnight. We follow the beam of Matt's flashlight between the headstones.

The Devil's Chair is built into a low brick wall that surrounds a private burial plot consisting of two graves. One of the headstones has toppled over while the other is missing entirely, and the chair sits facing the graves. According to information Matt gleaned from the Internet, the chair is a mourning bench built by a man who wanted a place to sit while visiting his wife's grave. A symbol of love, not evil. But in the dark, the bench lit only by the shine of a big summer moon, I half expect to see the devil waiting there for us.

"What time is it?" I fall back to clutch Noah's hand as

Matt points the flashlight beam at his watch. I'm not usually scared of things that go bump in the night, but Joan's warning creeps out from the corner of my brain where I've kept it tucked away all afternoon. What if there's someone out here, lurking in the woods, waiting for urban-myth chasers like us? Thinking about the gun in Joan's premonition makes me shiver, and Noah wraps his arm around my shoulder.

"We've got a couple of minutes," Matt says. He places an unopened can of beer on the armrest of the big brick chair, an offering for the mythical devil who is supposed to drink it without opening the can—or, more realistically, for the person who will come along for the free beer after we leave. "Who's going to sit?"

"Count me out," I say.

"Aw, come on, Cadie." Noah catches me up against him and pulls me down with him onto the chair. Straddling his lap. His hand steals beneath the back of my shirt, and his mouth grazes my neck, making me shiver for a whole different reason. "I won't let the devil get you."

"You guys . . ." Matt sounds irritated.

"How do I know you're not the devil?" I whisper to Noah, my lips touching his. I can feel his smile against my mouth, even in the dark.

"Better the devil you know than the devil you don't," he whispers in reply as his fingers tiptoe up my back.

Matt counts down the seconds. ". . . Three . . . two . . . one . . . midnight."

Noah kisses me at that moment, holding me so close I can feel how much he wants me. His face is rough with stubble under my palms, and his tongue warm and alive in my mouth. I sink so quickly when I'm around him, turning into an aching, hungry creature more frightening than any devil could be. And it isn't until the sound of a revving engine splits the stillness around us that I realize we're alone. Several of the buttons on my shirt are open, and Matt is gone.

"Shit." Noah laughs, holding me on his lap as he digs in his pocket for his phone. It rings a long time before kicking over to voice mail. "Dude. Matty, come back," he says. "We're sorry, okay? Come back and get us." His shoulders sag as he disconnects the call. "We could be in for a long night."

"He's not coming back?"

"I wouldn't count on it," Noah says. "I don't think we took the Devil's Chair seriously enough for him, so he's probably gone off to sulk."

"What do we do now?"

"Well, we have two options. We can walk back to our campsite, which will probably take a couple of hours from here," Noah says. "Or we could just stay until morning."

"The idea of sleeping in a cemetery scares me a little."

His big warm hands cover my back as he kisses me. "We don't have to sleep."

"Noah, I'm not—"

"I know." He kisses the tip of my nose. "You're not the kind of girl to have sex in a graveyard. But let me ask you this . . . what kind of girl are you?"

"What?"

"Look, anything I say at this point is going to sound like I'm trying to get in your pants," he says. "Which I am, but not because you're some campground conquest. I really like you, Cadie." Noah's lips find mine in the dark again. "But if it happens right here, right now, we're the only ones who will know." He must be aware of how persuasive his mouth—including the words coming out of it—can be, because the next time he kisses me, the tip of his tongue teasing against my upper lip, I feel boneless. Breathless. "It's not going to change you into anyone other than who you want to be."

Maybe it's a line. Maybe it's a lie. But I like this answer enough to take up where we left off, and it isn't long before heat races through me like a brush fire, burning me right up to the roots of my hair. I let Noah remove my shirt. "I draw the line at this chair," I say between kisses, as I tug his T-shirt up over his head. "It creeps me out."

He doesn't say anything. He just takes my hand and leads me away from the Devil's Chair, beneath a copse of trees where the ground isn't so sandy and we're not directly on top of someone's final resting place. I never pictured my first time would be like this—in a cemetery two hours from home. In my head it was always with Justin. Always in my own bedroom. And always on some hypothetical weekend when both my dad and Danny were gone.

Even in my imagination the odds were against me having sex.

But here I am, with Noah's discarded jeans and T-shirt serving as a bumpy barricade between the rough grass and my ass, and I straight-up want him.

"You, um—you have a condom, right?" I don't know why I'm whispering, but saying the words out loud in a cemetery seems . . . indecent. As if being completely naked is somehow not.

His lips move on my neck, sending a little shower of sparks through me. "Uh-huh."

"With you?"

Noah's soft laughter vibrates against my skin. "In my jeans, under your butt."

He lifts and shifts me, rummaging through his pockets until he produces the square foil packet. I feel strange watching him put it on, but I do and it's fascinating because even though I've seen Justin—and even Noah—naked before, I've never seen this.

When he's finished, he locks eyes on mine and I feel

him against me. And then inside me. It hurts a little at first. My knees tremble on either side of him, and my heart thumps with this terrible fear that I've made a mistake. Especially because he falls silent—his eyes bottomless dark and his face so serious—and I wonder if I'm doing something wrong. If he can tell I've never done this before.

But then he moves so gently, and almost all at once I lose the ability to breathe in a meaningful way. The everyday inhale-exhale method walks off the job, and over his shoulder the stars seem to explode out of the darkness and—no one ever tells you that your first time can feel good. But it does. And when a gasp slides out of my throat, Noah wraps it up in the sweetest kiss.

We dress in silence later—so much later that there is a hint of light in the still-dark sky—and I have no idea what time it is or what to think. Or what Noah thinks of me. And even though it's a weird moment and place to be thinking about her, I can't help thinking about my mom. Whether I would tell her about this. Wonder what she would say.

We had the sex talk back when I wasn't kissing Ray Buck. Girls at our church were taking vows to save themselves until marriage and wearing purity rings. Mom couldn't even sit through the pledge service without giggling, so she excused herself and went outside. Later, she told me that my virginity wasn't something to be lost or won, given or received.

"Your goodness doesn't lie between your thighs," she said, and my twelve-year-old blush was so furious I thought my face was going to explode. "And you don't lose value by having sex. When you are ready, Cadie, you will know it. Just be your regular smart self and you'll be fine. Also, never have sex with Ray Buck. He's as dumb as a post."

Noah buttons up his jeans and leans forward to kiss me, cradling my cheek in the palm of his hand. "Doin' okay?" he asks, and I like that he wants to know.

"I think so." But the truth is, I'm not completely sure. I *am* changed. My skin feels different. New. And I can still feel the imprint of him all over me. But here is what I know: I don't have to be in love with Noah. And having sex doesn't make me into someone I don't want to be. I'm not a slut and Mom was right. I'm still Arcadia Wells, ridiculously normal. "Do you think the dead mind? I mean, are we disturbing them?"

Maybe I'm not completely normal.

Noah wraps his arms around my head and rubs his knuckles across my hair. "What a weird thing to worry about," he says. "But no, I don't think they even know we're here. I don't believe in tarot or the Devil's Chair or any of that stuff, but if I did, I'd say they were probably happy that someone was getting laid instead of getting laid to rest."

Laughing, I trail my fingers up his side just above his

jeans, making him squirm—a weird new knowledge I have of his anatomy—and he drags me back down to the ground. Noah stretches out, crossing his legs at the ankles, and holds me against him. Kisses the top of my head. I close my eyes and feel the rise and fall of his chest under my cheek until we're breathing together. He tells me about the other places he's slept—abandoned warehouses, derelict houses, communal squats inhabited by his drug-addict friends.

"It beat living at home," he says, when I ask why. "My dad drank a lot, and I didn't like getting the shit beat out of me for no reason."

"Is that why your mom sent you to Maine?"

"Partly." The pause that follows feels weighted with more—with things he wants to say—but a yawn overtakes me and I feel his lips against my temple. "Go to sleep, Cadie."

"Noah?"

"Yeah?"

"I might be the kind of girl who has sex in graveyards."

His chest shakes with silent laughter, and he squeezes me gently against him. "I guess that makes you my kind of girl."

CHAPTER 11

CHAPTER 11

Matt is lounging in the Devil's Chair when we wake a few hours later, his leg thrown over the arm as if it's his very own chair. His hair is damp at the ends, and he's wearing another plaid shirt from what seems an endless supply. This one is primarily brown and does really nice things to his eyes. His mouth curves into a sly little grin, as if he knows what I'm thinking.

"The beer is still here," he says. "My illusions have been shattered."

"Sleep well?" Noah asks.

"Like a baby. You?"

"Ground was a little hard," Noah says. "Otherwise, okay."

Swiveling my attention from cousin to cousin, I

wonder whether an explosion looms on the horizon, but both of them are grinning as if one abandoning the other at midnight in cemeteries is a common occurrence. So very different from the knock-down-drag-outs Justin and Jason would have over minor things, like eating the last slice of cheese or what to watch on the TV in the back room.

Matt stands and hands Noah the keys to the Cougar. "I walked Molly."

"Thanks, man."

"You're welcome." Matt drops his arm around my shoulder as we walk toward the car. He smells nice, too. Clean. "Cadie, did you know there's an actual town in Florida called Arcadia? We should go there."

"If you want. There's nothing really there, though. Cattle farms, orange groves, a one-street main drag like back home in High Springs." He opens the door for me, and I climb into the back with the dog. It's so comfortable after sleeping on the ground that I stretch my legs between the front seats, my heels resting on the console. "The Peace River is close, but other than that . . ."

"We are here for the camping." Noah drops into the driver's seat and tickles the bottom of my dirty foot—he's as familiar with my terrain as I am with his—and my face gets hot. He grins at me in the rearview mirror as he starts the engine. "Maybe we can paddle downriver from Arcadia to the Gulf."

"It's a pretty long way, and then we'd have to go back for the car," Matt points out. "But we could paddle as far as we can in a single day, camp overnight on the river-bank, and then head back the next day."

"Done," Noah says. "Cadie, you in?"

"If I can have a hot shower, a change of clothes, and breakfast," I say, "I'll go anywhere you want."

On our way through Cassadaga, we pass Joan's house with the purple neon hand glowing in the front win-dow. She comes out of the house with a little boy. As she locks the front door he does these weird little toddler hops—the kind where he tries to get both feet off the ground, but actually only gets one at a time. It's some-thing I remember Daniel Boone doing when he was learning to hop, and I feel a longing so ferocious it brings tears to my eyes. I lean forward, my face between the seats. "Can I borrow a phone? I need to call home."

"Yeah, sure." Matt opens the glove compartment and as he rummages through registration papers and CD cases, I decide I'll call Duane first. Feel him out to see if Dad is still as mad as he was yesterday. Then I see some-thing that brings Joan's warning slamming back into my head and everything else is just . . . gone.

"Whose gun is that?"

Lots of people I know own guns. Justin's dad owns an entire arsenal of hunting rifles displayed in a bizarre china-cabinet-for-gun-collectors in their family room.

Duane keeps a gun in his tow truck—just in case. Even my father has an unloaded gun locked in the safe in his bedroom closet. But a medium in Cassadaga didn't warn me about those guns.

"It's mine." Noah says the words matter-of-factly. There's no pride or shame in his tone, just his own Noah-ness.

The gun looks like something from an old-school police show, and even though Joan didn't describe the gun from her premonition, I can't help imagining this is what she saw.

"Cadie, are you okay?" Noah pulls the car onto the shoulder of the road and puts it in park. "You look completely freaked."

"Why do you have a gun?"

"There are all kinds of dangerous things you can run into out in the Maine woods—bears, bobcats, a pissed-off moose"—he smiles at me, and I think that's my cue to respond, but laughter is very far away right now—"and even not-so-good people. I've never needed it, but I can put it in the trunk if it would make you feel better."

"It would," I say, although I'm not sure anything about the gun is actually going to make me feel good. But right there on the side of the road with me watching, Noah unloads enough of the trunk to have access to the spare and hides the gun inside the gray-checkered spare tire cover.

"Hey." After the trunk is reloaded, he touches my chin to get me to look at him. It's hard to do when I don't know what to think about all of this. "I was hiking Mount Katahdin once, and I met a black bear on the trail. She was fat and lazy and ready to hibernate, so she didn't even bother with me. I got lucky. Another time I was camping alone near the coast when I was approached by a hobo looking for food. He turned out to be a harmless dude with amazing stories, but both those things made me realize I had to be more prepared. I don't want to carry the bulk and weight of a rifle, so . . . Cadie, you don't have to be afraid of me."

"It's just—yesterday, the psychic's premonition—she saw a tattoo and a gun."

"What kind of tattoo?"

"Not one of yours," I say. "But—"

"Look, there's no good way to say this, but do you think maybe you're overreacting a little bit? I mean, you're putting a lot of stock in the word of a woman who makes up prophecies for a living in a town founded by a man who believed he was led here by ghosts."

I laugh, mostly at myself. "When you put it like that . . ."

"I swear to God, Cadie, I will not hurt you." Noah doesn't try to kiss me, which is a huge relief considering my nerves are still a little jangled. He just touches my arm with gentle fingers and walks his way along the side of the car to the driver's door. He looks back at me as the door hinge creaks open. "You in?"

I've never had an issue with the fact that my best friend keeps a gun for protection when he's making roadside assistance calls along I-75, so why can't two guys camping their way through a strange state do the same? Florida is full of weirdos—most of them natives. Running my hand through my hair, I look at Noah standing there looking at me. He's waiting for an answer, and I am a sucker for his face all over again.

So I get in the car.

CHAPTER 12

C adiebug, where are you?"

Duane doesn't sound mad when I call him from the road, but he doesn't sound especially pleased with me, either. I press a finger to my ear opposite the phone to blot out the rush of the wind.

"Down around Arcadia," I say. "We're planning to do some canoeing on the Peace River."

"Is Lindsey Buck with you?"

"She left yesterday morning before I even woke up," I say. "Texted that she had a family thing and needed to go home."

"Her mom got a message saying she was with you."

"That's weird."

"Very," he says. "A camper's gone missing up in

Okefenokee Swamp, Lindsey's not answering her phone, and you're off traipsing around Florida with a couple of strangers you met at a party. So you might be able to understand why your dad is a little crazy right now. Truth be told, I'm a little worried, too. You doing okay?"

I've got Molly's head resting on my thigh, and Noah looking at me in the rearview mirror as he drives. "Couldn't be better."

"As long as we've been friends I've known you to have a stubborn streak," Duane says. "But what's up with this little rebellion? This ain't like you."

"I've only been gone two days," I say. "Dad should be able to manage for two lousy days. I'm tired, Duane, and I hate being made to feel like a selfish bitch over this when I just want to feel like a regular teenage girl again. Even if it's just for a few days."

"When you coming home?"

"Tomorrow," I say. "We're going to paddle as far downstream as we can make it in one day, camp overnight, then head back. I promise."

"If you want, I can come pick you up," Duane says. "Maybe bring Daniel Boone along for the ride."

"Maybe." I probably should have said those things to my dad instead of unloading them on my best friend, but it's nice to get them off my chest. "I'll call you."

"Be safe," Duane says. "And if you hear from Lindsey, let us know, okay?"

"Okay."

It's closing in on noon by the time we're on the water. Noah paddles solo, carrying his dog and a pared-down collection of camping gear, while Matt and I share the second canoe—him in back, me in front, and the big red cooler in the middle.

"I think we're going to get wet," Noah says, as we head side by side up the Peace River from the landing at Gardner, a few miles north of Arcadia. The water is the same tea-stained brown as the Santa Fe back home. A little narrower. Not quite as shady, although the same kinds of trees line the bank. The current is slow and lazy this time of year so paddling upstream is not hard work. But clouds are thickening in the sky and the bright blue of this morning is working its way toward gray. I think he's right.

"There's a landing with a campground at Zolfo Springs," Matt says. "It's about thirteen miles, and as long as we don't get lightning we can paddle in the rain."

"Do you think you'll be able to handle that, Cadie?" Noah asks.

The extent of my experience includes my river picnic with Justin, a two-hour trip I did with my dad when I was a kid (he did all the work), and our visit to Naked Ed the other day. But a hopeful look hangs on Noah's face, and I want to prove to him—to both of them, really—that I can do this. That I can keep up. "I guess I will."

Noah's blue-ribbon smile makes me feel as if I've won a contest, and I wish we were together in one canoe, but Matt's been like a third wheel since Lindsey bailed. It doesn't seem fair to make him do everything alone. It's not his fault she's gone.

"Hey, Cadie." I turn around at the sound of Matt's voice. He takes off his Red Sox baseball cap and leans forward in the canoe to drop it on my head. "This'll help keep the rain off your face if it comes to that, and I have a spare rain jacket in my pack."

"Will you be okay without it?" The cap is warm and damp with sweat around the band, but the bill throws shade across my face. He knots a blue bandanna around his dark hair. With a day's worth of stubble along his jaw and his hair off his forehead, his resemblance to Noah is profound. They could be brothers.

"I'm good." Matt winks, and I spin back forward, heat crawling up my neck. He laughs softly, but I don't turn around.

The river is quiet. There are no other boats on the water, so ours are the only voices we hear. We use them sparingly, comparing our progress to the landmarks we pass or asking for another bottle of water from the cooler.

We snack on trail mix and point out deer, herons, or the alligators that stare at us with cold eyes. But mostly we just listen to the creak of the trees, the rolling rattle of gopher frogs, and the rustling of wild turkeys that pay us no mind at all as they forage the riverbank for bugs and seeds.

Matt gives a low whistle as we pass a large tom. "Man, what I wouldn't give for a shotgun right now."

"Right?" Noah agrees. "Turkey dinner over an open fire."

The mention of a shotgun calls to mind the handgun in the trunk, and I wonder if Noah is wishing he'd brought it along. Maybe he did. I study the contours of his back, wondering if the gun is stashed in the waist of his shorts under his T-shirt like they do in the movies. Or maybe it's buried in his duffel. Can you even shoot a turkey with a handgun? "Did you bring—"

"I brought a pack rod." Noah interrupts before I can finish the question, but I get the feeling he knows what I was going to ask. "Maybe we can catch some fish for dinner."

"That sounds really good." I don't know whether I'm relieved to change the subject or bothered that he didn't answer my question, but I don't ask again. Maybe I'd rather not know if he has the gun. "If you'll clean them, I'll cook them."

"Deal." He grins, and I wish for the millionth time that we were in the same canoe. The distance between us isn't that much—a few yards, maybe—but all I want to do is touch him. Which is both exciting and scary. I don't remember feeling like this with Justin. Not even at the beginning when we were all secret smiles in classes and stolen kisses at my locker. Noah has discovered things about me that Justin will never know. That I didn't even know until last night.

We've paddled for several hours, and the afternoon sun hangs low in the sky, when we reach a stretch of river-bank where the forest thins to grazing pastures dotted with cattle. A handful of cows drink along the river's edge and a pair of gangly-legged babies—their nubby horns peeking from behind tan-colored ears—frolic along the bank, following us.

Molly's bark rings sharp and clear, startling me. "She's been so quiet that I completely forgot she was here."

"She's like that sometimes," Noah says. "But it's about time for her to have a run. Once we get away from the cows, we'll take a break."

"We've got to be getting close to town." Matt speaks for the first time in a while. "Why don't we just head there so if it starts raining we won't be stuck in the middle of nowhere."

The canoes drift along together, bumping gently

against each other, as Noah consults the map from the canoe outpost. "Zolfo Springs is still a ways off. We'll just stop for a couple of minutes to let Molly blow off some steam."

My butt is sore from sitting all afternoon and I've had to pee for the past hour, so the prospect of stopping sooner rather than later is appealing. "I wouldn't mind a break."

Matt doesn't look happy about the decision but he doesn't say anything. He simply digs his paddle into the water and our canoe pulls ahead.

We haul the boats onto a sand-and-grass island in the middle of the river. Molly leaps out of Noah's canoe but she doesn't just run. She goes crazy, zooming around the island in wide circles. Splashing into the water. Rolling in the sand. Noah gets out an orange Frisbee with chew marks around the edge and sends it sailing. Molly leaps high off the ground, snatching it right out of the air. Over and over he throws the Frisbee for her and never once does she miss, even when Noah flies it out over the river.

Leaving my clothes on the bank, I wade out into the water and sink down to my neck. A tiny part of me is embarrassed because it's obvious I'm going to the bathroom, but it's such a sweet relief to pee that I don't even care. When I'm finished, I stretch out on a patch of grass to let my bathing suit dry. My arms ache from paddling, there's a dime-size blister at the base of my middle finger, and I'm exhausted. The sky is darker now and the clouds have closed in the gaps. And I'm praying for the rain to come down hard so I don't have to leave this spot.

"You guys go on without me," I say, as Matt drops to the ground beside me. "I'm just going to die right here, okay?"

He shoves the ball cap down so it covers my face. "Tired?"

"You have no idea." I don't bother pushing the cap back up because the darkness on my face feels good and it hurts to lift my arms. "I am having more fun than I've had in a really long time, but I am not a wilderness girl. You guys make it seem way more easy than it is."

"Yeah, but we have years of experience," Matt says. "I mean, the first time my parents took me paddling was before I could walk. And Noah eats, sleeps, and breathes wilderness. If that *Into the Wild* dude knew half the shit we do about survival . . . well, he might not have wound up dead in a bus."

"You won't catch me testing that theory, though," Noah says, and I feel the heat of his body as he sprawls out on my other side. When he lifts the cap off my face, his smile is the brightness in a cloud-dark world. "Hey, you."

"Hey, yourself." I smile back and my heartbeat kicks up a notch as he leans down to kiss me. His lips are warm and salty from sweat—and he smells like wet dog from letting Molly jump up into his arms—but it doesn't stop me from bringing my own aching arms up around his neck to pull him closer. We haven't touched all day and I just want him against me.

Our mouths are a breath apart when I'm hit in the forehead by a big fat raindrop that trickles down my cheek like sweat. Lightning flashes across the sky over his shoulder, white-hot and jagged.

"Shit." Noah falls back on the grass. The three of us lie there collecting the rain on our faces, our skin, our clothes, until the space between the drops gets smaller. Feels colder. "Looks like we're spending the night right here."

I was looking forward to Zolfo Springs. Maybe calling Dad to see if he's still mad. Finding out if Lindsey's made it back home. And maybe talking to Danny. But I'm too tired to even groan. Beside me, Matt gets to his feet and stretches out a hand to help me up. "We need to pitch the tent before it starts pouring."

We work as quickly as possible to unload the canoes and make camp, but by the time we dive through the tent flap, we're drenched. The rain drums relentlessly on the fabric over our heads and we sit in a soggy row—even Molly—watching millions of tiny drops dance on the surface of the river. Thunder rumbles the air around us, and each time lightning crackles it looks like the sky is being torn in two.

"So much for fishing." Noah peels off his T-shirt and throws it out into the rain-soaked grass since it can't really get any wetter. He leans back, propping himself on a rolled-up sleeping bag.

Matt nods. "No building a fire, either."

"Yes, but . . ." Rain spatters on my head and shoulders as I dig through the cooler—just outside the tent flap— grabbing beers for Noah and Matt, Coke for me, and a plastic baggie of slightly watery cheese cubes. My hair is dripping again when I pull back inside. "If the crackers are dry, we've got ourselves dinner."

Noah laughs a little. "Damn, Cadie, so fancy."

"I know, right? You should see what I can do with a box of macaroni and cheese and a pound of ground beef." I hand him an only-a-little-bit-damp cracker with a cube of Colby Jack on top, and he pops it into his mouth. "I'm practically Betty Crocker."

"My mom used to cook the meat with a packet of taco mix and then add the mac and cheese." Noah opens his beer and foam bubbles out, cascading down the side of the can and dripping all over his already wet shorts. He doesn't miss a beat. "If we had a jar of jalapeños, she'd throw those in, too."

"Yep." I nod, arranging the crackers and cheese on a

paper plate as if we are somewhere nicer than a too-crowded tent in the Middle of Nowhere, Florida. "My little brother loves it, too."

"Well, yeah." Noah smiles. "That shit's delicious. Of course, Matty doesn't know about the wonders of ramen noodles and boxed mac and cheese. Kid's first solid food was lobster served with a silver spoon."

Matt's eyebrows push together and the atmosphere in the tent feels hot and thick, and I'm pretty sure we're not really talking about food anymore. Seems odd that Noah would hold a class grudge against the people he's lived with the past several years. Or maybe he's trying to paint Matt in a not-one-of-us light because he's still jealous. Matt doesn't say anything, and I wonder if he's still mad that Noah wouldn't listen to him about Zolfo Springs. He just takes a long drink of beer and extends his middle finger at his cousin.

"I'm kidding," Noah tells me. "Except his mom makes the real thing and uses like eight or nine kinds of cheese, and sometimes she really does put lobster in it. Seriously legit."

"I could go for some of that right now." I throw a smile at Matt—a small solidarity—but the equilibrium still feels off. It seems like they're both angry about nothing, but I don't know their buttons and bombs. I probably never will. We fall into an uncomfortable silence and just sit awhile, watching for signs the rain is letting up and munching damp cheese crackers.

Noah falls asleep with his head on the sleeping bag and his legs crossed at the ankles. Molly slinks behind me and curls up between his arm and his side. I smile to myself, only a tiny bit jealous of the dog and only because I know how nice it is right there in that spot.

"You know what I could go for?" Matt says, as if our long-abandoned conversation was still going. "Pie."

"Oh, yeah," I agree. "Banana cream."

"And apple."

"Rhubarb."

"Chocolate cream."

"Key lime." We say that last one at the same time and laugh together. I glance at Noah to make sure we didn't wake him, but he's still sound asleep with his arm flung over his eyes. His mouth open slightly. His face is relaxed, making him look younger than he is. Not so tough. Kind of adorable.

When I turn back, Matt has a sly grin on his face, and I have a feeling he's plotting something. "I don't think we're as far from the town as he thinks," he whispers. "Let's paddle up, walk into town . . . I mean, there has to be someplace that serves pie."

"But it's raining."

"It's stopped."

"We should wake Noah," I say, but Matt shakes his head.

"No." He slowly unzips the screen on the tent. "We shouldn't."

I feel guilty for leaving Noah behind, but I rationalize it away by telling myself he's tired from having to paddle alone today—even though I know that's not even remotely true. I was the one dying on the riverbank while he was entertaining a cabin-fevered cattle dog. It might not be as adventurous as sex in a graveyard, but I like the idea of a clandestine pie run.

The air is swollen with moisture and the ground is squishy beneath my bare feet as we run down to the canoes in the fading light, but Matt is right—the rain has stopped. A slight breeze rustles trees, and it sounds as if rain is still coming down, but overhead slivers of sky peek between the clouds and the glow of the rising moon lurks just behind the bottom of a retreating thunderhead. The frogs and crickets are crazy loud now, masking the sound of the canoe scraping along the sand as we push it into the water.

Matt and I make a silent getaway, not daring to speak for five minutes, ten minutes. Not until we pass under the State Road 64 bridge and round a little bend that puts us at a park on the edge of Zolfo Springs.

"Damn it," Matt swears softly, as we carry the canoe

up the paved ramp and turn it upside down on the grass. "I knew we weren't that far away. We could have had dinner in a restaurant instead of cooped up in the tent."

"I don't mind." I stash our paddles beneath the boat and slide my feet into my flip-flops. "I kind of like our little island."

"Of course you'd side with him."

"It's not about sides." We walk through a wooded campground and past a pioneer village museum with old-timey buildings and a steam engine. If anyone was around, they'd probably think we were homeless, our clothes having dried on our bodies and our hair flattened by rain. Sand and gravel have worked themselves between my toes and my flip-flops, and once again I'm in desperate need of a shower. "It would have been cool to camp here, but whatever. We're engaged in Operation Clandestine Pie, Matt. You and me."

I wait to be rewarded with a laugh, but when it doesn't come right away, I wonder if there was something in the rain that soaked into their skin. Turned both him and Noah into testosterone monsters. But then a smile splits Matt's face and he laughs, lifting his fist for me to bump, the same way he did the first time we met. "Locked and loaded."

CHAPTER 13

CHAPTER 13

We find a family-style restaurant across the street from the park. It's nothing fancy, and the place is deserted except for a couple of guys drinking coffee at the lunch counter, but they have pie. An older waitress seats us at a booth with a clear view of a television silently broadcasting the news.

"Can I get you something to drink?" she asks, placing plastic-covered menus in front of us on the table.

"Couple of Cokes?" Matt looks at me to check if that's okay, and I nod. "And we don't need menus," he says. "We'll take one slice of every kind of pie you have."

Her going-gray eyebrows shoot up. "Every kind?"

"Yep."

"Hon, we have six."

"I know."

"This some kind of joke?" Maybe she thinks we're the dine-and-dash type. The Kendrick brothers and I tried it once at the IHOP in Lake City, but I snuck back to pay for our food. It was busy that morning, and we weren't even gone long enough for our waitress to notice we skipped out, but I still felt bad. Maybe she was a single mom or weighed down by debt. What if IHOP made her pay our bill?

Matt leans to fish his wallet from his back pocket and slaps a hundred on the table. "Will this cover it?"

"Well." The waitress sighs as if she still thinks we're pulling some sort of scam on her, but Matt flashes her one of his sweet smiles—he's so good at those—and her demeanor softens. The corner of her mouth twitches. "All right, then."

"And could we please have some sound on the TV?"

She doesn't acknowledge the request, but after putting in our order for six kinds of pie, she takes a remote from under the counter and unmutes the television.

"I need to go attend to some business . . . in my office," Matt says, as he slides out of his side of the booth. "Save a little pie for me, okay?"

He heads off to the men's room, and I turn my attention to the television.

". . . and finally, a tragic ending in the search for a

Florida man who went missing Tuesday in Georgia's Okefenokee National Wildlife Refuge," the newscaster says, as a white banner at the bottom of the screen declares Missing Florida Man Found Dead, and I wonder if that's the missing guy Duane was talking about this morning. "The body of twenty-four-year-old Brian Patrick Clark was discovered this morning by park rangers. The Jacksonville man, who relatives say was camping alone in the park, was reported missing after he failed to return home last weekend. Cause of death has not been issued, but park officials say Clark was found with a single gunshot wound to the head. No suspects have been named, and Clark's death remains under investigation."

"Such an awful shame," the waitress says as she places our Cokes on the table. "What kind of person would do such a thing?" She stands there for a moment, looking up at the television as if the answer will appear, then sighs. "I'll be right back with your pie."

Thinking about how Brian Patrick Clark's family must be feeling right now makes me think about my dad. There's some small comfort in knowing Duane ran interference for me. Dad knows I'm okay and that I'll be home soon. As much as I'd love to go to Flamingo with Noah—and spend every last possible second with him until he heads off into his real life—I need to get back. I miss Danny. I even miss Dad.

"So what's happening in the real world?" The booth seat squeaks as Matt returns.

"A whole lot of nothing."

He picks up his fork and taps the tines on the paper placemat in front of him. "So, Cadie, are you going anywhere for school?"

My grades weren't great, but good enough to be admitted somewhere. Except Mom left such a hole in our lives that I just stopped thinking about college. My guidance counselor encouraged me to apply. She even gave me the applications, but I had Danny to worry about. And Dad. So the applications sat in my desk drawer until the deadlines passed. They're still there now.

"I haven't really figured out what I want to do yet," I say. "I'm—well, I'm kind of handy with a sewing machine, so—okay, don't laugh, but I thought maybe I could start my own shop."

Justin used to lie on my bed while I stitched secondhand clothes into new patterns—skirts, tops, and I even tried my hand at shorts once—but I never told him about this private dream. Now that I've told Matt, it's out of my head and into the universe. He doesn't make fun of me, though, and I'm happy about that.

"It's just that I don't have much money," I say.

"Have you thought about selling your stuff online?" Matt asks. "You'd have barely any overhead, you could do it from anywhere, and people love handmade shit. Not that what you make is shit. I'm just saying that's what I would do."

He turns his attention to the TV, where contestants are questioning their way through *Jeopardy!* answers, as I sit here wondering why an online shop never occurred to me, especially considering how much of my life I've wasted on the Internet. Dad dipped into my meager college fund to pay Mom's hospital bills, so I don't have enough to pay for even a semester of college. But I do have enough for a new sewing machine and probably enough to set up a virtual shop.

"Thanks," I say, and Matt looks back at me as if he's already forgotten the conversation. "For the online idea. It's a good one."

He winks. "I'm handsome and smart."

"So after your camping trip in Florida, what are you going to do?"

"I go back to college in the fall."

"Where?"

"Yale."

I tie my straw wrapper in a knot. "That's pretty impressive."

"I guess. I don't know. Yeah." Matt shrugs like getting into an Ivy League college is nothing special. There might be a few kids from my high school who were admitted to

Harvard or Yale, but most everyone I know is going to a state university or joining the military. Or not going anywhere at all.

"Smart and handsome," I say, which makes him grin.

The waitress comes up to the table bearing a tray filled with plates of pie—apple, cherry, banana cream, chocolate cream, pecan, and, of course, key lime—and we line them up in a row on the table between us.

"Which one should we try first?" I ask. "Should we have a plan or just go for it?"

Matt severs off the point from the slice of cherry and forks it into his mouth, talking around the pie. "Don't overthink it. Just eat."

I decide to sample them in order, least favorite to favorite, starting with pecan because I hate pecan. He shakes his head as I wash the offensive taste down with a big mouthful of Coke.

"Why eat it if you don't like it?" he asks.

"I want to be fair."

"Life is too short, Cadie." He extends his arm across the Formica-topped table, bringing his fork to my lips. Speared to the end is a bite of key lime pie. Tasting it will throw off my system because key lime is my all-time favorite, but the last time a cute boy fed me pie was never. "You have to take what you want."

I open my mouth to accept the bite he's offering, and

his gaze is a bonfire on my face as he watches me chew the sweet-tart pie. I'm overcome with the same need to flee that I felt the time he kissed me. Not because the way he stares bothers me, but because it doesn't. And it should. Shouldn't it?

"It's too bad Lindsey didn't stick around." I focus on the plate of apple pie sitting in front of me. "I wonder if she made it home okay."

"Do you want to call home?" Matt digs his phone from his pocket and glances at the screen. "Or, maybe not. No signal."

"Weird."

One of the men at the lunch counter is talking on his cell phone, telling someone a loud story about the cracked exhaust manifold on his Ford Ranger. Matt's gaze follows mine. "I've had spotty coverage since we've been in Florida," he says. "That's what I get for not going with the nation's largest network, huh?"

"We are pretty much east of nowhere," I say. "And I've lost signal walking from the kitchen to my bedroom, so—"

"If you need anything else, let me know." The waitress drops the check on the table, and Matt slides the one-hundred-dollar bill on top of it without bothering to look. I don't think he does it to impress me, but I have to appreciate that he can afford to make that kind of move without a second thought.

"A box," he calls after the waitress, as we survey the leftovers—the crust ends of half a dozen types of pie. "We'll take the leftovers back to Noah as a peace offering."

The guilt I left back at the campsite catches up with me, and I'm sorry we didn't invite Noah to come with us. "Do you really think we need to make peace?"

"I don't know," Matt says. "Maybe. He might think we stole the Cougar and headed to Flamingo without him. He can be kind of . . . volatile."

I've known them only a couple of days, but "volatile" seems like too strong a descriptor. I mean, threatening Jason, getting jealous over Matt, and whatever general crankiness he was suffering back at the tent—those things aren't insignificant but they're also not volatile. "Really?"

"Well, okay, he's pretty much kept himself in check since he came to live with us. But you know about his . . ." Matt gestures at his forehead in the spot where a scar would be if he were his cousin. I nod, even though Noah didn't share the whole story. I only know the boot-to-the-face part. "And that part of his sentencing was to get anger management counseling?"

"Sentencing?" He told me he was defending himself so my own naive imagination spun up a scenario in which poor young Noah was the victim. I assumed the other guy deserved it. But now . . . the victim might have been someone he knew. At the very least someone who could pick him out of a police lineup. Someone who pressed charges. "Who—?"

"Shit, Cadie, I figured he told you everything," Matt says. "I shouldn't—you should probably talk to Noah about this. It's not my place."

"Who was it?"

"He, um—okay. He attacked his dad. Put him in a coma for three days. Noah did a few months in juvie, but got a reduced sentence in exchange for counseling. And then his mom sent him to us to keep him away from his dad."

"Absentee." "Drunk." "Son of a bitch." Those were the words Noah used to describe his father. Could his dad have done something to deserve being beaten into a coma? Is there a crime that deserves such a punishment? *"I will fuck you up."* Those were the words Noah said to Jason. Is that the kind of person Noah really is? The kind of person who will fuck you up? How much of what he told me about his life is really true? How many lies might I have believed?

The questions make my head feel too heavy for my body, my eyes tired. I rest my forehead on the table. I don't know how to respond to this new—and unsettling—information.

"I'm sorry I told you," Matt says quietly. "Noah has

come a long way, you know? We're all really proud of him."

"We should probably take him the leftovers," is what I finally, stupidly, say. Because, no, I don't really know how far Noah Thomas MacNeal, age twenty-two, has come. "Just in case."

CHAPTER 14

When our little island comes into view, Noah is there, roasting fish like hot dogs on sticks over the open flame. If he's spent the past couple of hours simmering with rage, he hasn't been idle about it. He watches silently as we pull the canoe onto the bank. We're greeted by wood smoke, the scent of cooking fish, and Molly—her tail furious with happiness—as we make our way up to the fire. And still Noah says nothing.

Matt bypasses his cousin—who sits on a fallen tree that he's dragged from God-knows-where—and wades across the shallow water between the island and the opposite bank, then disappears into the woods. I sit down beside Noah on the tree. Not as close as before, and I wonder if he notices.

"So, uh—where ya been?" he asks. His tone is casual but my ear is now tuned for anger. I don't hear it, and handing him a Styrofoam box of half-eaten pie feels like a crappy apology for not inviting him along. Especially when he's been hauling logs, building fires, and catching fish.

"We went for pie."

Instead of opening the box of leftovers, Noah rotates the fish to keep them from burning. In the firelight his face shines golden and it doesn't make sense that I still want to kiss him when my stomach is a jumble of bees. "Everything okay?"

"Yeah. Fine." I'm not sure if it's the truth. "Why wouldn't it be?"

"I don't know, Cadie." He blows out a frustrated breath. "Maybe because you took off with Matt and—"

"It wasn't like that," I interrupt. "It was just something to do."

"Without me."

"Don't be jealous."

"I'm not."

"No?"

"Okay, maybe a little." He grins and rubs the back of his neck the way Duane does whenever he's about to say something that's going to be sweeter than he wants to admit. "Matt can be impulsive and reckless sometimes. I was worried, is all."

Words plus gesture turn my insides to Marshmallow Fluff. Despite everything Matt told me, Noah still has the power to unravel me. "I'm sorry I didn't wake you."

He touches his forehead to mine. "Me, too."

"Are you mad?"

"Should I be?"

"No."

"Then . . ." He kisses the tip of my nose at the same time his fingertips skim a strand of hair behind my ear. A tiny thrill follows his fingers and continues on down my spine. ". . . we're good."

Noah digs into the pie, eating with his fingers, as I look at the roasting fish. Their unseeing white eyes seem to stare back in a way that unnerves me. I'm confused. And I'm having trouble making this Noah—the one who kisses me with a sweetness I've never tasted—mesh with the one Matt described.

I pull in a deep breath and slowly exhale, trying to prepare myself for the question I'm about to ask. "Did you put your dad in a coma?"

"Yes."

The word sits on the air a moment, and I'm not sure what to do with it.

"But my dad is not a decent human being," Noah says. "He is an abusive asshole."

He removes the fish from the fire and stakes them, upright, into the ground so they'll cool. Molly lifts her head off Noah's boot to sniff the air and lick her chops, but relaxes when he tells her no. He reaches down to pet her head.

"I was a pretty wild kid," Noah continues. "I ran with a tough crew. Did drugs. So if it was just me . . . there were times I deserved to be knocked around. But one night I came home and caught him with his hands around my mom's neck. I punched him to get him off her, and he smacked me in the head with a tequila bottle. I was so high I didn't feel it. So high that I just kept on hitting him until he was on the ground, and after that I kicked him and kicked him and—" There's a catch in his voice and Noah blows out a sharp breath as if he's trying to keep from crying. "I would have killed him if Mom hadn't pulled me off, but I swear to God I didn't mean for it to go that far."

"Matt didn't tell me you were defending your mother. He just said you were volatile."

"What would you do if someone hurt your brother?"

Noah's question gives me pause because there is no limit to the damage I would inflict on someone who tried to hurt Danny, but before I can answer, Matt comes sloshing his way back across the river from the trees.

"If a bear shits in the woods and there's no one around to smell it, did he still shit?" he says. "The answer, in case you're wondering, is yes, and the bear recommends staying upwind of it."

Noah laughs as he reaches into the cooler and tosses Matt a beer. "Have you heard about the new movie *Constipation?*" Noah waits a beat. "Hasn't come out yet."

He and Matt crack up like a pair of six-year-olds, reminding me of my little brother, who is only just starting to discover potty humor.

"Okay, I've got one for you," I say. "Why did Tigger stick his head in the toilet?"

"Ooh, I know this one!" Matt points a finger at me. "He was looking for Pooh. What's brown and sticky?"

Noah shrugs. "What?"

"A stick."

The air between them seems cleaner, and I wonder if they just needed a break from each other. They've been together since their grandmother's funeral in Savannah. Noah offers me the next beer out of the cooler, but the thought of drinking makes me tired. "I'm going to bed," I say. "Today has caught up with me."

He catches my pinkie finger and tugs me gently toward him. "You okay?"

I nod. We've all been on top of one another since we left O'Leno, so even though the softness of his finger around mine makes me want to drag him off into the tent, I'd rather be alone. For a while I lie listening to their low and unintelligible words, their quiet laughter, and the *whoosh-crack* opening of beer cans. These are the sounds of Noah and Matt righting whatever was tipped over. Going back to who they are without me in between.

I wake when Noah crawls into the tent on all fours, grabs a sleeping bag, and backs out again. I don't know how long I've been asleep, but it feels like only a few minutes. Except Molly is pressed against me, belly-up and legs in the air. I watch through the open flap as Noah spreads the sleeping bag over a sound-asleep Matt and then comes back to the tent.

I close my eyes as Noah curls up behind me, his warm skin smelling like smoke and sweat and maybe even the rain itself. My body shifts from soft with sleep to wide-awake want—and I'm surprised by how quickly it happens. Even without him saying a single word.

"Are you awake?" he whispers as his arm steals around my waist. "Because I really want to kiss you."

"Is that all?"

His laugh is low and warm on the back of my neck. His lips follow his breath, and my nerve endings light up with pleasure. "If you want to do more, I'm not going to say no, but—"

"Are you drunk?"

"A little bit . . . maybe . . . definitely . . . yes," Noah admits with a thick-tongued slur, and I know I was asleep longer than I thought. "But I want to kiss you all the time. When you smile. When you're pissed off and fierce. Just—it doesn't even make sense because I just met you three days ago."

"It doesn't." I shift to face him. His arm is already around me, his fingers splayed on my back. He presses me gently against him. Legs. Knees. Hips. Chests. "Because you scare me and it doesn't stop me from wanting to kiss you, too."

"Cadie, you don't have to be afraid of me." His mouth is so close I can almost taste his words. "You've got me so twisted I can't even think straight, but I would never hurt you. I promise."

Promises are easy to believe in the middle of the night when it's dark and just us. When his kisses burn my lips and the stubble of his hair feels soft against the palms of my hands. When the movement of his hips steals my breath. And when I fall asleep with my head on his shoulder, I have the fleeting thought that tomorrow—or maybe it's even today by now—is going to be a very long day on the water. But every minute, every kiss, will be worth it.

The next time my eyes open, I'm face-to-face with a still-asleep Matt, who must have come inside in the night. The heat of four bodies in one tiny tent is oppressive, and the rain is unrelenting. There are no two ways about it; this day is going to be miserable.

We are spared the thunder and lightning of yesterday, but the sky spits rain at us all day long. Sometimes it comes as a downpour, other times it's a mist that gets in our eyes and clings like a second skin. There is nothing to see except the endless splatter of drops on the river. Molly burrows beneath one of the thwarts of Noah's canoe, but it doesn't keep her dry. Nothing is dry. Even our food is soggy, but we eat it anyway. And we don't talk because there's nothing to say about how tired, hungry, and saturated we are. We just look at one another with weary eyes and paddle like robots, over and over for hours, as if it's the only thing we know.

This is insane.

And not just paddling twelve twisty miles of Peace River in the rain.

What am I doing here?

I haven't talked to my dad in two days. He's probably moved from worry to sheer panic because I haven't come home. And maybe he's right to be afraid. Maybe I should be more afraid. I had sex with a guy I barely know. Followed him into the middle of nowhere because of it. Even after I found out about the gun. Even after Lindsey didn't go home. He swears he won't hurt me, but his past tells a different, violent story, and I don't know what to believe. I rationalized everything, telling myself that I earned this time away from home. But now, with too much time to do nothing but think, I wonder if I was just plain selfish. Just . . . stupid.

By the time we finally paddle up to the beach at Gardner, the blister on my hand has swelled, shredded, and bled. The skin on my fingers is so wrinkled it hurts. I stumble getting out of the boat, fall onto the sand, and just stay there, crying with relief. Crying from the pain. Crying because I want to go home. I stay there until Noah helps me to my feet. My legs are rubbery from sitting too long, sand clings to my shins, and I feel as if I'm in an unfamiliar body as we walk to the Cougar. Matt is already at the trunk, rummaging through the bags for dry clothes.

I'll get my stuff and then I'll call home. Duane will come. My vision blurs again as I think about how he will drive three hours for me, no questions asked.

"Are you okay?" The concern in Noah's voice twists my insides. The pull toward him is so strong, even when I don't want to feel it.

"Yeah. I don't know. I think—" I stop short, not wanting to tell him I'm leaving. Not wanting to look at him for fear of changing my mind. He's like a sickness, a craving, and I want to believe the best about him, even when the worst has been crawling around inside my brain all day. "I need to call home."

"Yeah, sure." Water drips off Noah's duffel as he scoops it from the bottom of the canoe and hands it to me. "My phone's in here somewhere. Get dry. Call home. Matt and I will meet you at the car after we get the boats on the trailer." I nod and as I walk away, he says, "And, Cadie, if you want me to take you home, I will."

I change into my clothes in a tiny stall in a primitive bathroom, where the toilet is just a hole and the air smells like shit and chemicals. My clothes are as wrinkled as my fingertips, and they're not exactly clean but they're mostly dry. After being so wet, I can live with a little dirt and a bit of damp. I wring the water from my hair with paper towels and then unzip Noah's bag, searching for his phone. I push aside a green flannel shirt, and stuck between the folds is a map of Okefenokee National Wildlife Refuge with a campsite rental receipt stapled to the corner. The date stamp on the receipt puts Noah and Matt there at the same time as the guy who went missing. The coincidence sends a creeping uneasiness down my spine.

I dig deeper and find the phone at the bottom of the bag. Dial. Wait. It rings only once before Dad answers.

"Oh, thank God." The words rush out of his mouth as if he's been holding them there in reserve. "Cadie, where are you?"

"We just reached Gardner," I say. "We've been on the river since—"

"Are you okay?" The underlying note in his voice isn't

anger. Or even worry. It's fear like I haven't heard it since just before Mom died. Even though he knew she was dying, he was afraid. For her. For himself. For all of us.

"Yeah, I'm fine. What's up?"

I can hear the wrongness in the way the line goes quiet except for the soft inhalation he always takes just before he's about to say something I don't want to hear. But I also hear a tiny hitch in his breath, and fear bubbles up inside me. "Cadie, Lindsey is— The rangers at O'Leno found Lindsey Buck's body this morning."

"Her body?" His words make no sense at all because finding a body means Lindsey is dead. "What?"

"She was left in the woods," Dad says. "Tied to a tree with a clothesline and shot, um—she was shot in the head."

"But she texted me and said she was—oh, God." I sit down hard on the dirty toilet seat as the tumblers align in my head. Tied to a tree. Like Jason Kendrick. Shot in the head. Like Brian Patrick Clark. By someone with a gun. *Don't give him your heart. He will break you.*

"Cadie, are you safe?"

"I don't know."

"Just tell me exactly where you are." Dad's voice is calm now. Comforting. And I explain that the landing is down a small dirt farm road off Route 17 between Zolfo Springs and Arcadia. "I'll come get you. Stay put, okay? Promise me."

Lindsey is dead.

"I promise."

This time when the line goes silent he's gone, and almost immediately I want him back. I want him to promise me in return that everything will be okay when it feels like my life has broken free from its own gravity and is spinning wildly away from me. But it will be okay. I will wait right here in this bathroom stall until it's safe for me to leave.

Except there's someone knocking on the door, and a lady's voice asks if I'm almost finished.

"Just a second." I grab Noah's bag, and the contents spill onto the bathroom floor. Lying amid the shirts and shorts is another phone with a pink rhinestone case.

Lindsey's phone.

My heart is beating so hard and fast that I can hear the blood rushing in my ears. Feel my body pulsing with it. What do I do? I can't stay in the bathroom, but I don't want to go out there. The lady knocks again, and my time is up.

I stuff Noah's clothes back in his bag, shove both his phone and Lindsey's in my pocket, and throw the latch on the door, stepping into a world that's grown too bright. Matt stands beside the door. His clothes are clean and dry, and his still-damp hair curls around his ears. There's a little spot of sunburn peel on his earlobe. He looks too much like Noah, but I'm scared and I don't want to be alone. Exposed.

"Cadie, are you okay?" he asks.

I'm alive and Lindsey is dead. I'm so far from okay that I don't even remember what it feels like. "No."

"I know today was tough with the rain and all," Matt says. "But—"

"Lindsey is dead."

His mouth drops open for a moment. "What?"

"They found her body in the woods at O'Leno." Those particular words coming from my mouth spin surreal into real, and tears start sliding down my face at a pace I can't control. "She was tied to a tree like Jason, but she was—" I draw in a shuddering breath. "God, Matt, I promised Mrs. Buck nothing would happen to Lindsey. I promised."

"Shit." He plows his fingers through his hair. "I should have seen this coming. I should have—shit, Cadie, I should have known better."

I wipe my face with the sleeve of my T-shirt. "We need to call the police."

"We need to get the hell out of here." He reaches into the pocket of his shorts and pulls out the keys to the Cougar. "Now."

"Where is, um—where is he?" I can't even bring myself to say Noah's name. My stomach twists as I think about the night in the cemetery. About last night. How good he was at pretending, and how thoroughly I fell for it.

"He's in the bathroom," Matt says. "I say we leave now and call the police on the way back to High Springs, okay?"

"My dad told me to wait for him."

"Do you really think he'd want you here alone with Noah?"

"No, but I promised—"

"Come on, Cadie." Matt looks over his shoulder at the door to the bathroom. He looks as freaked out as I am as he extends his hand. "I don't even want to be here alone with Noah. We need to go. You can explain it to your dad on the way. I swear."

I slip my hand into his.

"Okay."

CHAPTER 15

CHAPTER 15

Noah comes around the corner from the men's bathroom side of the building as we're driving out of the parking lot. I know because I turn around to look. I can't read his expression from this far away, but he doesn't run after us. He doesn't shout or kick at the dirt or throw something at the car like they do in movies. Noah just stands there with Molly at his feet, watching us leave him behind. A trickle of sentiment runs through the evidence against him. How can that boy—the one who touched me so gently, the one whose dog follows him around as if he's a god—be a killer?

Noah jams his hand into his jeans pocket as if he's going for his phone, and I remember it's in my pocket. I pull it out and press the button to wake it up. There's nothing unusual about his phone. Useful apps. Sensible apps. Weather. Maps. Hiking. Camping. Paddling. Music. Photos. I touch my thumb against the photo gallery icon. I don't know why I want to look or what I expect to find. Maybe that one thing that proves all of this wrong. That will turn him back from monster to human.

The first image that comes up is one of me at the campfire party, standing by the beer trough in my dress and motorcycle boots. It seems like a lifetime ago. I linger over the picture a moment, wishing I could rewind time and go back to being that girl. Or even the one before her. The one who might have stayed home.

I slide to the previous image, and my heart lodges in my throat. It's Jason, tied to the tree, with his head lolled over to one side and tape on his mouth. It's dark around the edges and bright near the middle like it was taken at night with a flash—and it's close enough to see tears on his face. My eyes sting, and I slide away from the photo, not wanting to look any longer.

The next photo brings fresh bile into my throat. Same pose. Clothesline. Duct tape. But there is a tattoo etched on the man's chest in red and gold—a flaming Sacred Heart like the one in the psychic's vision—and a bullet hole in his temple. I've never seen this man before, but I would bet everything I own that his name is Brian Patrick Clark.

Dread rises up in me as I slide to the next image.

It's worse.

So much worse.

It's Lindsey.

She's posed just like the others, tied up and gagged with duct tape, but her dead eyes are wide open. I close my own but I can still see the negative image of her naked body behind my eyelids. Any doubts I had about Noah shrivel like paper in fire, my heartbeat goes crazy, and salty saliva fills my mouth. "Stop the car."

"What?" Matt's attention turns from the road. "Cadie, what's wrong?"

I push the phone at him, and after a beat the car slows until we're stopped at the side of the road. The door groans as I fling it open and stumble a couple of steps to the grass, where I fall on my knees and vomit until there's nothing left inside me. I stay there a moment—eyes watering, nose dripping, tiny bits of gravel digging into the meat of my palms and the bony part of my knees—wishing I were safe at home in my room, imagining adventure instead of being trapped in this nightmare. A sob crawls up my throat and bursts out into the air, and all the tears I've been trying not to cry come out with it.

I feel Matt's hand on my back.

"It's going to be okay." His voice is as gentle as his touch, and I let him help me to my feet. I'm crying so hard I can't speak as he guides me back into the car with his arm around my shoulder. Matt fastens my seat belt and closes my door, then walks around the front of the car, his fingers pressing numbers on Noah's phone. Calling the police.

A couple of minutes later he gets in the car and negotiates the Cougar back on the road. "Noah is stuck at the landing without a car," he says. "And the sheriff's department is sending a deputy. He can't hurt us, Cadie. It's going to be okay."

"Don't they need to question us or something?"

"I gave them our names." Matt steers the Cougar back onto the road, and we head north on Route 17. "The officer said they'd contact us if they need us to give statements." He hands me back the phone, and I call home. There's no answer on the landline, but Dad is probably on his way so I dial his cell phone. It goes straight to voice mail.

"Hey, it's me," I say. "I know I promised to wait for you, but I didn't feel safe. I'm on my way home."

To the west of us lies the river we just paddled, as Matt and I head toward Zolfo Springs. If I never visit this part of the state again it will be too soon, and the anticipation of going home makes me cry all over again.

By the time he pulls into a gas station, my whole body hurts and my eyes are thick and swollen. I lean my head against the window as Matt pumps gas, and I try to imagine my little brother's smile. Justin's true-blue eyes. My mom's face. Anything to keep from closing my eyes and seeing Lindsey's lifeless stare. Anything to keep from thinking about how terrified she must have been just before Noah shot her in the head.

"Here." Matt hands me a paper coffee cup as he drops back into the driver's seat. "Hot chocolate. Thought it might make you feel better."

"Thank you." The first sip scalds my tongue, but I'm so numb with sadness that I don't even care. The engine turns over with a growl and again we're back on the road. "Did you know he was capable of doing something like this?"

Matt sighs and takes a drink of coffee, his eyes fastened on the road ahead. Reflexively, I mimic the gesture and burn my tongue again. A tear leaks out of my left eye. When it reaches my chin, I use my shoulder to wipe it away. "My family—" he says finally. "We all knew Noah was capable of something like this, but we were fooled into believing he had it under control."

"Had what under control?"

"On paper they call it antisocial behavior disorder," Matt says. "He lacks impulse control. He lacks empathy. But what it means is that he's—well, he's a sociopath."

"Why—" As if this nightmare couldn't get any worse, I feel like my brain just exploded inside my head; my thoughts are a scrambled mess. "Why would you even hang out with him?"

"I thought—"

"You saw what happened to Jason," I interrupt. "And you didn't immediately suspect Noah? Or maybe you did and failed to mention it. Either way, you just let Lindsey and me come along knowing Noah was dangerous. Why would you *do* that?"

"He's my cousin," Matt says quietly. "My friend. He's been like normal for so long that I wanted to believe he was okay. And I wanted—I don't know. I wanted you around, even if you didn't like me the way you liked him."

"Lindsey is dead and here I am." I hold up my arms like I'm a game show prize. "Was it worth it?"

"Cadie, don't—"

"Don't what? Don't feel guilty because I dragged Lindsey into all this and your cousin murdered her? Don't feel like an idiot because I had sex with him? Don't feel too stupid for words that I'm still in the car with the guy who knew something like this could happen and didn't do anything about it?"

"Look, you think I'm not completely freaked out?" Matt's voice is sharp. He runs his fingers up through his hair, and his driving hand squeezes the steering wheel. "Do you think I want to admit that someone who lived in my house, ate breakfast at our kitchen table, played with my little sister, and slept in the bedroom next to mine could actually kill someone? Fuck no, Cadie. I wanted to believe Noah was functional. And that if I was with him nothing would go wrong."

"Yeah, well, it's gone light-years beyond wrong."

"I know," Matt says quietly. "I know."

I turn away from him and look at the world rushing past the window as we drive in silence. The landscape appears the same as it ever was, but it's different now. Alien and strange. Or maybe that's just me. I drink more hot chocolate—no longer as hot—and silently ask my mom to set the world right again. Make this all a mistake. She doesn't answer, so I think about how she used to put colored marshmallows in my cocoa when I was small. Which is an odd thing to think about, but the memory floats warm and hazy through my brain.

"I swore the green ones tasted different." The words sound like they're being said in my own voice, but it isn't until Matt gives a little laugh and asks me to repeat myself that I realize I've actually spoken aloud. He sounds like he's a million miles away from me and I feel woozy. As if I'm going to be sick. "Stop."

Gravel crunches beneath the tires as Matt pulls the car off the road for a second time. My fingers feel thick and uncooperative as I fumble with my seat belt. Hanging over the edge of the door frame, I wait for my stomach to convulse and for the sour burn in my throat, but nothing happens. I close my eyes, and the darkness is a relief.

"Cadie." Matt eases me back upright. "Are you okay?"

"I'm just—" I blink. God, I'm so tired. "Matt, I want to go home."

"Okay." He nods as he reaches past me to pull the door closed, then strokes his hand down the back of my hair. It feels so nice that I want to burrow my head under his palm and maybe put my head on his shoulder. "I'll take you home, Cadie. Just . . ."

He says more words but they sound far away and faint, as if he's talking from the other end of a long tunnel. I close my eyes again, and the words just stop.

I wake to sticky eyelids and a hangover ache as if I've been drunk. I don't know how long I was asleep but it feels like a very long time and I don't remember dozing off. My head is too heavy for my neck, and I prop my elbow on the edge of the window to hold myself upright. The first thing I notice are the headlight beams pushing out into the darkness, illuminating scrubby trees and a narrow two-lane road that doesn't look like any road I've traveled before. The sky stretches out around us forever, inky blue and riddled with more stars than I've ever seen.

The Cougar races down this nowhere stretch of road,

and a yellow diamond-shaped deer crossing sign is no help at all. My heart hammers double-time as I ask, "Where are we?"

Matt leans toward the steering wheel as if shifting his body forward will get us there—wherever "there" is—faster. The tires squeal as we speed around a curve, and I grip the door handle. He's grinning when he finally looks at me, but it's no longer sweet. No longer kind. "About five miles from Flamingo."

"But—"

Realization wraps a cold hand around me and threatens to drag me under. There was a picture of me at the campfire party on Noah's phone. I was standing by the beer trough, wearing my dress and boots. Before we went skinny-dipping. Before I met Noah. They have identical phones. Identical waterproof cases. Except in Noah's photos, my hair would be wet and I'd be wearing his Trojan All-Stars T-shirt. "Oh my God. That's your phone."

"Yep."

And the other photos—the ones of Jason, Brian, and Lindsey—were manipulated. Rearranged to devastate me and make me believe.

"Noah didn't—" My mouth goes dry with fear. Matt is driving me to the barely inhabited tip of Florida where—oh, God. How did I get this so wrong? "He didn't kill Lindsey. He didn't kill anyone, did he?"

"Nope." So casual, his tone. With a hint of pride.

I slide my hands beneath my thighs to keep them from shaking. "Why?"

"The guy up in Georgia was practice." His shrug is constructed of utter disregard. "But Lindsey was just for fun. She was irrelevant."

"Lindsey wasn't irrelevant."

"Oh, please. She was a pain-in-the-ass little backwoods hick."

"Like me?"

"Lindsey was a means to an end. When you said you'd come with us, her time ran out," he says. "But you—you're still useful."

"Oh, well, that's a relief." My sarcasm falls flat when my voice trembles, but Matt laughs anyway.

"See, this is why I like you, Cadie," he says. "You're brave, even when you're sitting over there terrified that I'm going to kill you. And you're smart to be scared. I probably will."

I consider jumping from the car, but even if I survive the impact without breaking myself, we're still forty miles from anywhere. Flamingo is a town that has the Everglades creeping in on it from three sides while its back is pressed against the Gulf of Mexico. I could escape Matt but get lost in the vastness of the glades and die of starvation. Or be eaten by an alligator.

"Pretty shitty odds, huh?" he says, and I'm startled we're both thinking the same thing. "You should just wait for Noah to try to rescue you—and he will because he's got this weird white-knight complex, you know? So the odds still won't be good, but they'll be better."

"Why are you doing this?"

"She left him the car."

"Are you fucking kidding me?" The words explode out of me, and even Matt looks startled. "All this is because your grandmother gave him a car? You're insane."

His arm shoots across the car, the back of his hand making contact with my mouth. My lips sting from the slap. "What the—"

Matt slaps me again. "Stop talking."

My lower lip throbs with pain, and when I lick it I taste blood. I do what Matt says. Partly because I'm afraid he'll hit me again, but mostly because I'm afraid he'll do worse.

CHAPTER 16

As we drive through Flamingo, I realize it isn't as deserted as I'd imagined. There is a fairly new marina and a visitors' center—both closed for the night, so there's no hope of finding refuge there—and a vacant campground. But at this time of night and at this time of year, when tropical storms threaten the coastline, Flamingo might as well be a ghost town.

Matt bypasses the well-lit center and drives down a darkened road to what used to be a neighborhood. There are concrete pads where houses once stood, and the few remaining homes are buttoned up for hurricane season. No streetlights. No cars.

I am alone at the end of Florida with a boy who plans to kill me.

A hysterical laugh bubbles up my throat.

Matt's head whips in my direction, and I shrink into the farthest corner of the front seat, pressing against the door, for fear he's going to smack me again. He doesn't. He just gives me a self-satisfied smile, as if I'm the unruly dog he's beaten into submission. He pulls into the gravel driveway of what was once a waterfront home site, and a thin line of mangroves is all that stands between us and the beach. Matt fiddles with the radio dial, trying to get a sharper signal on the country music filtering through the speakers. My hand is on the door latch, and I consider getting out. Running away.

Matt slides his hand beneath the driver's seat and pulls out Noah's gun. "You can run if you want." He gestures at the door as if I'm free to go. "I like shooting at moving targets. I'm pretty good with rabbits and squirrels. The neighbor's poodle was a challenge, but I got him, too."

I slump back against the seat and blink about a million times trying to keep from crying. Matt's phone rings. He pulls it from his pocket, smiles at the screen as he places it on the dashboard, and turns on the speaker function. "Perfect timing."

"What the hell, Matt? I've tried calling a million times. Where are you?" Noah's confused voice comes out of the phone, and hope snakes through my veins. I seize the opportunity.

"Noah, we're in Flamingo! Call the police!"

Matt's hand comes across the car again, splitting my swollen lip wider. My face burns, and the metallic tang of blood seeps into my mouth.

"Before you think about calling the police," Matt says, "you should decide if you want Cadie's death on your head. Because if the police show up here, I will kill her." Matt presses the snub-nosed barrel of the gun against my temple. I freeze in place, not wanting to do anything that might make his finger slip on the trigger. Tears course down my cheeks and snot dribbles from my nose, but I don't dare wipe them away. "She's been really brave, Noah. Give her a sporting chance. Come alone."

The line is silent, and I pray to God, to my mom, to anyone in the heavens who might be listening, that we didn't lose signal out here in the middle of nowhere.

"What's going on, Matty?" Noah sounds calm, and even though I'm shaking so hard the barrel of the gun presses against my skin over and over and over again, I'm somehow comforted by the sound of his voice. "Why are you doing this?"

"He wants the car." I turn my face quickly toward the window so Matt can't hit me again. The gun touches the back of my head, and I can hear the scratch of the barrel as it rubs against my hair. I pinch my eyes shut tight, but still can't help picturing my brains splattered against the window.

"It's yours," Noah says. "Done."

"It's already mine." Matt's voice is dead calm. "Every summer when I was a kid, Granddad would take me for a ride in this car and tell me that someday it would be mine. That stupid old bitch willed it to you, but it's my car. Someday is here."

"You have the Cougar, Matt. Just let Cadie go."

"Not until you get here."

"I'm already on my way," Noah says, and I wonder how. Is someone driving him? Where did he find a car? Is he close? "We'll talk, okay? Just don't— Cadie, I'll be there soon."

"No cops." For just a moment Matt sounds young and desperate, and I think maybe he's afraid of Noah. After all, if a fifteen-year-old Noah could damage a grown man, what might this Noah do to Matt? But the coldness returns to Matt's voice when he says, "I already killed Lindsey. I won't think twice about killing Cadie."

"No cops," Noah repeats. "I promise."

Matt touches the button to end the call, and the phone sits there on the dashboard. I lunge for it, and he pushes me away, cracking the side of my head against the window. Not hard enough to break the glass—or me—but pain radiates through my skull. I don't even know who I could have called. Even if Dad drove the whole way to the canoe landing at Gardner, he's still too far away to help me now. Duane can't come rescue me. And if I keep doing stupid things like this, maybe Noah won't even make it in time.

"Goddamn it, Cadie! Stop making me hurt you."

"Is that how it works? It's my fault?" My voice is thick with tears. "Did Jason make you hurt him?"

"He needed to be taught a lesson about respect," Matt says. "He got what he deserved, but you were too stupid to see it as punishment. You felt sorry for him."

"What about Lindsey? What did she do wrong?"

"Nothing." Matt smiles at me, and my stomach turns inside out. I can't help wondering if his lies about Noah were truths about himself. Sociopath. Psychopath. Murderer. Monster. No matter what the label, there's something very wrong with Matt.

He grabs the phone and the gun and gets out of the car, slamming the door closed.

As he stands in the beam of the headlights, my eyes dart to the ignition. Shit. The keys are gone, too.

I think again about running, but I'm not certain I could reach the hiking trail that lies beyond him before he shoots me, and I'm not sure where the trail even leads. The water is closer, but how long—or where—could I swim before I was too exhausted to go on? Are there sharks in those waters? I don't know, but the threat of alligators is very real out here in the Everglades. The smartest option—which is, admittedly, not a smart option at all—would be to run to one of the houses and try to hide. But even if I could get inside, if Matt finds me, I'll be trapped. If this was all part of his plan to kill Noah in a place where it would take weeks for his body to be discovered—if ever—it's a terrifyingly brilliant plan.

My head goes in circles for a long while, trying to figure out how I can get away from Matt, until my mind snags on Jason needing a lesson in respect. I get out of the car and comb my fingers through my tangled hair. There's absolutely nothing sexy about me at this moment, but it might be the only weapon I have.

Matt is leaning against the hood of the car, watching the road. Waiting for Noah.

"Hey, um—you know that whole thing with Jason?" I work on sounding a little bit shy and a little bit flirty, and I can't tell if I'm successful at either. "You did that for me?"

"Doesn't matter now."

"Of course it matters." I stand close enough beside him that we're almost touching. I keep my voice light and hope it's not shaking. "I'm sorry I didn't understand. Jason has always been a jerk to me, so I appreciate what you did."

Matt's eyebrows pull together, and his dark eyes register skepticism. Because I'm lying and he's not stupid. But I have to convince him I'm sincere. On his side. It's the only way I can think to stay alive until Noah gets here. The closer I am to Matt, the better chance I have of saving us both.

"It's too late for that," he says.

"Is it?" I lean beside him against the car. "I know you probably don't believe me, Matt, but I get it now. I do. Noah is a total loser who wormed his way right into your family and took everything that should be yours. Even I was fooled, but you were smart enough to see through it all."

"Exactly."

"I should have stayed with you at the party," I say. "But when I saw you with Lindsey I got jealous. Especially since I was the one who invited you. I waited for you, Matt."

"You picked him."

"Only because I thought you were blowing me off for her," I say. "And I'm still here now."

He laughs. "That's because I have a gun."

"Well, yeah," I say. "But I haven't made a run for it."

"Yet."

"Do you have any idea how much it sucks to be fourteen years old and raising a baby? I gave up my life to take care of my little brother." My breath hitches in my throat, and I have to pause to keep from crying because this isn't part of the charade. But the thing is, I would live this life all over again for Danny. "I'm just so damn sick of it, you know? Enough to run off into the wilderness with a couple of strangers."

I glance at Matt, and he's nodding. Maybe he's buying it. Maybe he's playing me. Either way, I forge on.

"You know, we could drive away," I say. "Go somewhere no one can find us. Change our names, change our realities, and drive a really spectacular car. How do you feel about Mexico?"

Matt laughs low, bumping his shoulder against mine—the shoulder attached to the arm attached to the hand that smacked my mouth out of its proper shape—and I try not to cringe. "It's a good plan."

"Then let's go." I push away from the car and hold out my hand to him. By the time Noah gets here, we could be gone. He'd be safe, and I'd have a chance to escape Matt somewhere other than the middle of the Everglades. It's risky, but it's all I've got. "Please."

Matt catches my hand and reels me back to him, pulling me between his knees the same way Noah did in my bedroom. Matt has the gun in his hand, so I know he still doesn't completely trust me as he cradles my face and brushes his thumb lightly across my swollen lower lip. He smiles a little, as if he sees my bruised face as some sort of trophy. My insides are a twisted knot, but I force myself to smile back, because this is a test and I have to pass.

Matt's lips touch mine, and when his tongue pushes into my mouth, I close my eyes and let it happen. The last time he kissed me it felt warm and sweet, but now there's a gun pressed against my lower back and the only way to get through this is to pretend he's Noah. Except Matt's mouth is invasive and demanding until I make a small sound—as if I'm enjoying it—and he eases up. He kisses the crack in my lower lip before he pulls back to look at me.

"This is so much better, Cadie." His voice goes low and soft, and for a moment he even sounds like Noah and I want to cry. "I like it when you cooperate."

Matt's hand moves from my face, sliding up under my shirt until his fingers meet the lower edge of my bra. My mouth tastes salty, as if I'm going to throw up, but when his hand worms beneath the cotton, I don't protest. My heart is beating so hard that I'm sure he can feel it pulsing through my skin. How far am I going to have to go to convince him I'm on his side? How far am I willing to go?

I tug at the front of his shirt with both hands, urging him down to the ground with me. Matt grins. It may be trust or it may be lust, but either way, his guard is lowered. The gun is pinned under his hand as he kneels over me, pushing up my shirt.

God, Noah, where are you? I don't want to do this.

Matt's movements are awkward as he tries to

unbutton my shorts with a single hand, so he jams the gun in the pocket of his shorts. I pull him down to kiss me, feeling the weight of the gun bump against my hip, and his hand slides up my stomach from button to breast. I tiptoe my fingers up his back, digging the tips into his skin so he thinks I'm enjoying this. I moan against his lips—

—and then I go for the gun.

CHAPTER 17

CHAPTER 17

Y ou stupid bitch!" Matt realizes what I'm doing almost immediately and grabs my wrist. We're still on the ground and I'm trapped beneath him as he squeezes my wrist so tight I'm afraid he's going to break it. "Did you really think I would fall for your pathetic seduction? And why would I stick a fucking gun in my pocket if there was a chance it would go off?"

"Why play along, Matt?"

"I wanted to see how far you would go," he says. "And it's easier than force."

He reaches into his pocket for the gun. With his other hand around my wrist, Matt's middle is exposed. I grab again, but this time I don't go for the gun. I grab his testicles through his shorts and squeeze as hard as I can. As hard as he's squeezing my wrist. Matt yelps in pain. Rolls off me. Lets go of my wrist.

I try to crawl away from him, to stand up. Matt lunges, his strong hand wrapping around my ankle. I kick back hard with my free foot, and there's a sickening crunch as the sole of my shoe makes contact with his nose. Involuntarily, Matt releases me, and I scramble to my feet, running as fast as I can toward the hiking trail. I still don't know where it leads, but Flamingo seems to be stretched out along the waterfront, so maybe it will take me to the marina and the main road down which Noah will come.

The crack of a gunshot rips through the air behind me, and the world slows, blood rushing in my ears as I wait for the bullet to pierce my body. How much will it hurt when it hits me? How many minutes will it take for me to die? Will my mother be there on the other side? But time speeds up and the second is over. Then the next one passes and I realize—Matt missed.

A second gunshot rings out, but I have an advantage now. I'm farther away. Beyond the fading beams of the headlights, becoming invisible as I follow the trail along the beach. I don't slow down as I listen for Matt. There is little tree cover, and my path is lit by the shine of the moon off the water as I dash past the deserted campground. I'm still a moving target but no more shots follow. It's unnerving because grabbing him by the balls couldn't have incapacitated Matt for that long. Why isn't he chasing me?

The trail funnels into a woodsy area just beyond an outdoor amphitheater, and I'm beginning to worry that I'm wrong about this path. I fear the silence. I doubt my own sense of direction, despite the Gulf being exactly where it's supposed to be. Through a break in the trees I see the remnants of another old neighborhood. A lone house sits at the top of the empty cul-de-sac. There are no cars in the driveway, but there are also no hurricane shutters sealing it up for the summer. Maybe the owners are just away. Maybe they have a phone I can use to call the police.

In the split second I make the decision to step off the path, I collide with something. Someone.

The beginnings of a scream escape me before a big hand clamps over my mouth and an arm wraps around my waist, pinning me tight against a wall of chest. I bite hard into the fleshy part of his palm as I struggle to break free, but he's too strong. I can't get away. I close my eyes and pray to my mom—or to any god who is listening—that my death will be quick. The answer is a *shhhhhh* sound beside my ear.

"Cadie, it's me." My body goes weak with relief as I recognize Noah's voice. He peels his hand away from my mouth. I can't see if there are teeth marks in his palm, but now that I know it's him, I hope I didn't draw blood. "I heard gunshots. Are you okay?"

"Yeah."

"Where is he?"

"He was shooting at me and I ran and—" The mangroves around us rustle slightly in the breeze, and panic slams into my chest. We're standing still. Easy targets. "We have to keep moving, Noah. I don't know where he is."

"This way." He takes my hand as if to pull me back the way he came—toward the parking lot.

"Matt's got the car, and he has to know this trail leads that direction," I say. "If we go the opposite—"

"He could be waiting for us at either end of the trail," Noah says. "But the parking lot is out in the open, and I have a truck waiting. We get to the truck and get the hell out of here."

I follow him down the path, leafy branches brushing against my shoulders like bony fingers, making me shiver. Fears pile up in my head as we run—especially the one that reminds me I trusted Matt to help me get the hell away and he brought me to this place instead—but I can't afford to give myself over to doubt. I focus on Noah's solid back and the feel of his hand around mine. On making it to the parking lot alive. On going home.

Light penetrates the spaces between the trees as we

near the mouth of the trail. Light from the Cougar's head-lights? Noah stops, and over the stillness I can hear an engine idling.

"Matt's watching the trail," he whispers. "Or at least he wants us to think he's watching."

"Should we go back?"

"He could be anywhere, Cadie," Noah says. "We have to run for it. I'll go first to draw him out. No matter what happens, do not stop." He folds a key ring with a single key into my hand. The key and the gentle squeeze that follows erase any doubt I ever had about trusting him. "Run to the truck and go."

"I'm sorry I doubted you," I say. "He showed me pictures of Lindsey and I thought—"

"Don't think about that now. Just go."

We hold to the darkest part of the path as we creep slowly forward to the end of the trail. Noah silently gestures forward with two fingers and bursts out into the parking lot. I run behind him and everything around me is a blur. I don't see Matt as I rush past the Cougar. I see only Noah in front of me and—some fifty-odd yards beyond him—an orange-and-white U-Haul pickup truck that would be hilarious if I wasn't so fucking terrified that I'm going to die before I reach it. Fifty yards is half a soccer field.

I can do this.

A gunshot cracks, and Noah is knocked out of his

trajectory. He falters, crying out in pain. His hand clutches his upper arm as I run past him. I'm closing in on the truck—thirty yards, twenty-five yards—when I hear Matt call out for me to stop.

"If you leave, I'll kill him."

"He's going to kill me anyway." Noah's voice carries across the lot. "Don't stop, Cadie. Not for me."

Twenty yards.

I stop and turn around.

In the amber glow of the parking lot lights I see Noah down on his knees with his left arm hanging limp at his side and Matt standing beside him with the gun pressed against Noah's head. Matt's face is darkened with blood from where I kicked him and his stance is soft from the pain in his groin, but he still holds all the power right beneath his trigger finger.

The smart thing for me to do is listen to Noah. Get in the truck. Drive away.

Live.

Except Lindsey's death hangs heavy on my conscience, and I don't think I can carry the burden of Noah's death, too. Even though it means I'm probably not going to make it home, I walk back toward them.

Matt's laugh is cold and sharp.

"I thought for a moment there that you were really going to leave." His words drip with condescension as he lobs them at me. "But in the end, you're just as predictable, just as weak, as everyone else. You let your stupid, useless feelings get in the way of what needed to be done."

"Yeah?" I lift my chin and take on the bravest, most arrogant tone I can manage. And, really, I don't have to dig too deep into my own emotional well to find anger. If I'm going to die, I'd rather be pissed off about it. "Well, what's getting in *your* way, Matt? You've got Noah on his knees and me—" I stretch my arms wide, making myself as big a target as possible. "Surely you can hit me now, can't you? Why don't you just do it? Or isn't that enough for your fucked-up ego?"

Noah closes his eyes, almost as if he's accepted our fate. But Matt doesn't shoot either of us. I don't believe it's because he has some tiny kernel of goodness left inside him, but for someone who wants Noah dead so badly Matt doesn't seem to be in a hurry to finish the job.

"Where's the fun in that?" he asks. "I want Noah to watch me skin his dog and violate you in all the best ways before I kill you both."

"Oh, God. Molly." My stomach goes into free fall.

Noah shakes his head. "She's not here."

"You never go anywhere without that dog," Matt says. "So what would make you leave her behind?"

"I called your mom," Noah says. "She told me. About you and her theory about Lily."

I look from one cousin to the other, wondering what a five-year-old girl has to do with Noah's dog. Or with any of this.

"There's no proof." Matt shrugs. "I didn't want a sister. It was easier to get rid of her when she was still a baby. Suffocation looks a lot like sudden infant death syndrome."

He talked about her as if she were alive. About her moobie star sunglasses.

"You killed—" My words drop away as my ears buzz and my head goes light, as if I'm going to pass out. My legs stop supporting me, and I sink to my knees in front of Noah. He cups my cheek with his good hand. "Stay focused, Cadie. Right here."

My eyes on his, I take a deep breath, trying to keep the darkness at bay. I touch my fingertips lightly against his left shoulder. The sleeve of his T-shirt is torn where the bullet ripped through it and blood blooms out from the hole in his skin.

"You should have gone," he says, his voice low.

"Then you would be here alone." I remove my T-shirt and use it to bind Noah's wound as tight as possible. There's nothing I can do if his arm is broken, but maybe the bleeding will stop. "Do you think I could just leave you behind?"

Noah touches his forehead to mine. "I'm so sorry."

"I'm so bored," Matt says, directing us to our feet with

a flick of the gun. "Launch one of the canoes so we can finish this game."

Noah rises slowly, and pain shadows his face. He's pale and unsteady from the loss of blood. I want to help him. I want to save him. Helpless fury swirls around inside me, and I consider tackling Matt. But even if I knock him down . . . then what? I wasn't able to get the gun away from him earlier tonight. Why on earth would I think I'd be able to do it now?

"What the hell is wrong with you?" I ask Matt, as I loosen the straps securing the boats to the trailer. I work slowly, hoping for . . . I don't know what I'm hoping for. The only sign of life in this place are swarms of mosquitoes drawing our blood at every opportunity. It's no wonder this town is practically uninhabited. It's uninhabitable. "Why would you do this?"

"This isn't going to end with a *Scooby-Doo* monologue about how my mommy didn't love me," he says. "Sociopathy isn't an affliction, Cadie. It's a gift."

"I doubt Lindsey Buck's family will see it that way."

"They'll never know."

"They will when you get caught."

"When your bodies are found—if they're found—it will look like your murder and Noah's suicide. The end to a tragic Florida killing spree," he says. "Complete with quotes from his distraught cousin about how I was always afraid something like this could happen and how I tried to stop him."

"Your mom will know the truth."

"She'll *suspect* the truth," Matt corrects. "But there won't be any more proof than there was with Lily. And she always keeps my secrets."

"Why?"

"Because she knows that if she tells anyone, I will kill her, too."

With a gun at our backs and Noah only able to use one arm, we carry the canoe to the launch ramp and slide it into the water. Matt follows behind us with a pair of wooden paddles.

"Ladies first." He motions for me to sit in the middle and for Noah to take the front. Noah can't paddle with just one arm and Matt is wielding a gun, so most of the paddling falls to me. I alternate strokes—left, right, left, right—as we move through the launch basin. Along the mangrove shoreline I see the dark, bumpy shape of an alligator floating on the surface.

Back in about second or third grade, a Florida Wildlife officer brought a four-foot gator to school. We thought it was funny that he carried it in a plastic dog crate and even funnier when it peed on the classroom floor. The alligator's mouth was bound shut with electrical tape to keep it from biting, and as we ran our fingers over its rutted hide, the officer explained the difference between alligators and crocodiles. Primarily, that alligators prefer freshwater and that crocodiles have narrower snouts.

I reach over the edge of the boat, dip my fingertips into the water, and touch them against my tongue. Salt. Even though I can't see its snout, I think the gator-shaped form must be a crocodile. They're rarer than alligators, and I've never seen one in the wild.

We pass through the narrow cut of the launch basin into Florida Bay and Matt points to the dark shape of a mangrove island up ahead. "Paddle there."

Every single day boats pass by that island. Fish and crabs live among the tangly mangrove roots, and birds nest in the branches, but there's nothing there for humans. No reason to ever stop. Noah and I will turn to sun-bleached bones without anyone ever finding us, and Matt will get away with it because no one will ever think to look for us here.

When I was little, my favorite bedtime story was *Scuffy the Tugboat*, about a toy boat who felt too big for the toy store that contained him. He goes from bathtub to stream to river to the edge of the sea, where he realizes that maybe there is a limit to his bigness. For most of my life I've ignored the part where—just as he's about to sail off into the vastness of the ocean—a hand reaches out and brings him back to the safety of the bathtub. Right here, right now, I'd give anything to be in my own bathtub with Daniel Boone on the other side of the door, telling me he needs to go potty. Because there's a good chance I won't make it home. And it may just be too late to hope for a hand that will bring me back.

Tears trickle down my face as Matt's words echo in my head—"you let your stupid, useless feelings get in the way of what needed to be done"—and I'm struck by a moment of clarity. I can't just paddle us to our deaths when I could do something. When I know what needs to be done.

It's too quiet on the water around us so I can't warn Noah. I can only hope that what I'm about to do doesn't make everything worse and that he will be okay.

The blade of the paddle drips across my shins as I lift it out of the water and bring it in front of me, as if I'm switching to the other side of the canoe. My heart beats so loud I can barely hear anything else. My hands meet in the middle, just as they normally would—one hand facing me, the other facing away. It's not a strong hold on the paddle, but it will have to do. I tighten my grip and draw in a deep breath. Shift my feet to the left and hope I can do this. Give a quick, matching half turn in my seat.

And swing as hard as I can.

CHAPTER 18

The edge of the paddle slams with a wooden *thwack* against Matt's head, just above his ear, knocking him sideways. I launch myself in the same direction, forcing the canoe to capsize. Spilling all three of us into the warm, dark water of Florida Bay. My body goes under completely and I'm disoriented until my feet find the mucky bottom and I come up standing. The water is torso-deep, shallow enough to stand.

Noah and Matt surface with me, gasping, and Matt lunges for the canoe. I realize then that his hands are empty. He must have dropped the gun in the boat. "Stop him!"

Noah tackles Matt around the waist and drags him under, both of them thrashing wildly as Matt struggles to free himself and Noah struggles to hold on. I push through the water to the swamped canoe and find the gun lying at the bottom, submerged in about a foot of water. I don't know whether a wet gun will fire, but I grab it anyway and turn around.

Under the light of the big summer moon, I can see that Matt has his hands around Noah's neck, pushing him underwater. Choking him. Drowning him. Noah pries weakly at Matt's fingers, trying to pull them away.

"Stop it!" The words come out louder, harsher than I expected, as fear turns to anger. With both hands tight around the grip of the gun, I lift it. Point it at Matt. "Let Noah go. Now."

Matt's laugh cracks like a whip as he lifts Noah's head out of the water but doesn't let go. "You're not going to shoot me, Cadie," Matt says. "The guilt will eat you up."

Except the life is draining out of Noah. His body is limp, his eyes rolled back in his head. I am not going to let him die. "If I have to live with the guilt of someone dying," I say, "it's going to be you."

My body jolts with the force of the first bullet leaving the gun, and the sound roars in my ears. Matt releases Noah on impact, staggering backward. I fire again.

And again.

I'm deaf to the click of the empty gun, but I feel it and I see Matt fall backward. He goes beneath the surface briefly, then bobs, floating faceup just a few feet from where Noah does the same. I close the distance to Noah. Curling my arms beneath his shoulders to keep his head above water, I haul him to the knee-deep flats.

"Stay with me, Noah." I sit down and hold him against me, my hand on his cheek. His skin is cool, and I don't think he's breathing. "You can't die now. Not after I saved you."

I learned how to do CPR when Danny was born—just in case—but I can't lay Noah down flat to perform chest compressions, and I don't know what else to do. I keep his head above the water and say a silent prayer that he starts breathing.

Noah's chest expands suddenly, rapidly, as he pulls in a sharp gasp. Breathing turns to coughing, and seawater spills from his mouth until his breath returns to something close to regular. Finally, he vomits.

"Are you okay?" The words sound as if they've clawed their way out of him. "Where's Matt?"

"He's, um—over there." Several yards away, Matt floats, unmoving, and I have no idea if he is alive or dead. Once I saw a movie in which a crazy woman pretended to drown in a bathtub. She lay beneath the surface with her apparently lifeless eyes open until her prey—and the whole theater—believed she was dead. We all screamed when she came surging up out of the water.

Leaving Noah in the shallows, I move gingerly toward Matt's body, the empty gun in my hand, terrified he's going to reach out and grab me by the leg and drag me under. There are two holes in his shirt—left shoulder and right chest—where I shot him, and bile creeps up from my stomach. His eyes stare up into the midnight sky like the woman's in the movie, but Matt doesn't surge. He doesn't take a breath. He is not faking. He is dead.

Four days ago I was a girl pulling off a minor rebellion by going to a campfire party in the woods. Now Jason Kendrick is broken, Lindsey Buck is dead, and I've *murdered* someone. The force of Matt's last words—"the guilt will eat you up"—hits me like a sucker punch to the heart. All of this is my fault.

A sob scorches its way up my throat. "I didn't mean for any of this to happen. I just—he was drowning you and—"

"Cadie." Noah is beside me now. How he can be upright, when my bones feel like they're going to collapse into a pile, is beyond me.

"I only wanted him to stop," I say. "I didn't mean to kill him."

"Keep it together." He wraps his good arm around me and holds me against his chest, his T-shirt wet against my cheek. It's only then that I realize we're holding each other up. "It's going to be okay."

"What am I going to do, Noah? I don't want to go to jail."

"That's not going to happen."

"But—" I try to close my eyes, but all I can see is Matt absorbing the blow of a bullet. Staggering. Falling. "I just kept shooting. And I hit him twice."

Noah releases me, reaches out, and tips Matt sideways. The way he handles Matt's body seems so disrespectful, and I have to remind myself that Matt left a naked dead girl in the woods. I think about her family having to see her like that. Matt doesn't deserve any better than this. Noah digs his hand into Matt's pocket and pulls out the phone. Pressing the on/off switch through the waterproof case, he brings the screen to life.

"We have evidence," he says. "And if anyone asks, we tell them I shot Matt."

"I can't let you do that."

"Look, I don't think either of us is going down over this," Noah says. "But if we're going to have a worst-case-scenario plan, I've been to jail once. I can do it again."

"They won't hire you for a national parks job."

"I don't care."

"I do." Maybe he is right. Maybe the fact that I killed Matt in self-defense will be enough. Maybe the photos on Matt's phone will be all the evidence we need. But even if Noah is wrong, I won't let him suffer the consequences for me. "We have to tell the truth."

The canoe has drifted since we've been in the water. It's close enough that I could swim to it, but the paddles are gone and we're too far from shore for the phone to pick up a signal.

"What happens now?" I ask.

"I'm pretty sure my arm is broken, so you're going to have to get the boat," Noah says. "We'll put Matt in there and—I don't know. I guess if we stick to the flats we can pull the canoe back close to the shore and then swim it the rest of the way in."

I'm already so mentally and emotionally broken that I don't think my body can take this, but the alternative is spending the night in the water with the body of the boy I killed. Crocodiles lurk among the mangroves and how long will it take before a shark smells Matt's blood in the water? It takes all my strength not to cry. "Okay."

I walk the flats toward the canoe until it gets deep enough to swim. The canoe is in the boating channel that leads out toward the ocean, but I don't have to worry about being run over when the world around me is almost completely silent. The only things I hear are my strokes cutting through the water and the sound of my breathing from inside my body.

I can do this, I tell myself. I can do this.

The swamped boat is heavy, and the returning takes longer than the leaving. I have to hold on to the side, paddling with one arm until I can stand on bottom again.

Pulling the canoe is easier, but by the time I get back to the flats, my arms and legs are crying in pain. I don't know how I'll be able to swim to Flamingo. Except I look at Noah—blood loss, broken arm, and nearly drowned—and dig for the strength to keep going.

Together, we invert the canoe to empty out the water. I turn toward Matt and see a narrow snout and a pair of dark reptilian eyes surface just beyond the body. The Florida Wildlife officer back in elementary school told us that alligators and crocodiles don't usually attack humans, but said that they can be opportunistic when faced with the chance for a free meal. And right now . . . I don't even want to think about what Matt's dead body looks like to this incoming crocodile.

"Noah." I keep my voice low. Steady. But really I'm terrified. "We have company."

"Get in the boat."

We climb carefully into the canoe as the crocodile— maybe the one from the shoreline, maybe a different one completely—tugs at the hem of Matt's shorts. The body dips gently below the water like a fishing bobber. The crocodile tugs again, this time a bit harder, with the same results. Meeting no resistance, the reptile opens its jagged-toothed mouth, clamps it around Matt's leg, and drags him under.

The ripples have faded and the water is serene before I speak. "Did that just—"

"Yes." Noah nods.

"What do we do now? I mean . . . Matt is *gone*."

"Well . . . it feels fucked-up beyond measure to say this, but I think our problems just got easier," Noah says. "You don't have to prove self-defense if there is no body, we still have the photos of Matt's victims for the police, and—"

"And Lindsey's family gets poetic justice."

It's so not an appropriate thing to say and it's even more inappropriate when we both start laughing, but I'm so far beyond normal right now that I don't even know what it looks like anymore. We laugh because if we don't I will have to look at Noah—sitting opposite me in the canoe—and remember that he is the same guy who stirred up something good inside me four days ago on the Magnolia loop road. We can't ever go back to that moment in time. And if there was a chance for something more than just this weekend together, what kind of future can there be for us now when death is what binds us? We laugh because otherwise I will cry.

Once the laughing has tapered to embarrassed-for-laughing silence, Noah runs his belt through the eye loop at the front of the canoe and we walk the flats—moving slowly because Noah is not okay—pulling the empty boat across the shallow water until we reach the mangrove-thick shore. There is still the matter of negotiating across the deepwater basin to the launch ramp.

"Get in the canoe," I tell him. "Let me do this part."

"No."

"You're barely standing," I say. "I don't want to have to worry about you drowning yourself when we've come this far. Just get in."

Noah agrees, lying down in the bottom of the canoe to equalize his weight, and I swim the rest of the way, towing the boat behind me. When I reach the shore, I have to wake him up to help me drag the canoe up the ramp and strap it back onto the trailer. It's still dark, but daybreak isn't more than a couple of hours away.

"So what now?" I ask.

"I need to take the truck back to Arcadia." Noah's voice is faraway and tired. There's no way he can drive a car. "And I left Molly with the lady who was in the bathroom at the landing. I need to get my dog."

"You need to go to the hospital."

"I can't," he says. "If I walk in there with a gunshot wound, they'll report it to the police."

"But—"

"Who am I going to say shot me, Cadie?" he says. "Matt's gone, and until we figure out how to handle this, the fewer people who know, the better."

Noah hands me his own phone, and when the signal finally connects, I find at least a dozen missed calls from my dad. I dial him back, and he answers before it's even stopped ringing.

"Dad, it's me."

I wait for him to yell at me for not staying in Gardner, but he doesn't. I just hear the rush of pure relief as he asks if I'm okay.

"I don't know." My adrenaline levels are crashing, and tears fill my eyes. "Where are you?"

"Eddie, Duane, and I are about ten miles inside the Homestead entrance to the Everglades," he says. "I didn't get your voice mail until we were already in Arcadia, and then I got a phone call from a guy named Noah who said he was on his way to Flamingo to find you. I didn't know whether we should trust him or not, but we—" His voice breaks, and I can tell he's crying.

"I'm so, so sorry," I say. "I was angry and—"

"We don't have to talk about this now." Dad's voice is so kind that I start crying in earnest. "Hang tight, Cadie, we're almost there."

"Come as fast as you can," I say. "We're going to need Uncle Eddie."

I wake in the backseat of the Cougar half an hour later to the *whoosh* of Jake brakes, and I've never been so happy to see Duane Imler's tow truck in my whole life. Beside me Noah's face is death-pale and cool to the touch, and I have to place my hand on his chest to make sure he's still alive. When I feel the soft rise and fall of his breath and the slow thump of his heart, I am awash with relief.

"Noah, wake up." I give him a gentle shake. "Help is here."

"No hospitals, Cadie." His words are sludgy as his eyes flutter open and then shut. "No hospitals, okay?"

I climb out of the car and step into Dad's arms. His embrace is the kind of fierce love I've been needing for the past four years, and I hug him back with all the strength I have left. "Oh, my sweet girl," he says. "I'm so sorry I've done such a terrible job taking care of you and Danny since your mom— I love you, Cadie."

"I love you, too, Dad, and we have a lot to talk about," I say. "But right now Noah needs Uncle Eddie. His arm is broken." I gesture into the car at the makeshift bandage knotted around Noah's upper arm. It's crusted with blood and stiff with dried salt water. "And there's a bullet in there somewhere."

Uncle Eddie joined the Navy after high school and spent ten years as a corpsman with the Marines. He may not have any medical credentials now, but everyone back home knows Eddie Wells is the man to see when you've caught your own hand with a fishing hook or your friend shoots you in the ass with a BB gun. He'll know how to dig out a bullet and stitch up Noah's wound. I'm not so confident about his ability to set a broken arm, but he pats my shoulder. "I've got this, kiddo."

As he and Dad examine Noah's wound, Duane loads

the U-Haul pickup onto his flatbed. When he's finished, he gathers me up in his arms.

"I'm so sorry," I say. "I don't even deserve you."

"Don't talk like that."

"Does everyone—does everyone back home hate me?"

"The Bucks are confused right now, Cadie," Duane says. "They're not blaming you, but they don't understand what happened to their daughter. They want answers."

This story is not going to stay contained. The Bucks need closure. The family of Brian Patrick Clark needs to know what happened to him. Even Matt's mother needs to know that the world is finally safe from her son. "I know."

Uncle Eddie comes over. "So the good news is that the bullet didn't hit anything vital," he says. "I've treated Noah for shock, but we really need to get somewhere I can take the bullet out and set the broken bone. It's not something that should be done in the backseat of a car."

"The sun will be rising soon, too," Dad says. "We don't want to be explaining all this to park rangers before we have an explanation. We need to go."

To the outside observer, we'd probably seem like a weird procession driving out of Everglades National Park. Except at this hour, there's no one around to see us. And if the desk clerk at the mom-and-pop motel just outside Homestead thinks it's strange that my dad is renting a room at five in the morning, he doesn't say so. It's the kind of place that also rents by the week, so maybe the clerk's seen his fair share of weird things.

Uncle Eddie and Dad half carry, half walk Noah into the room and stretch him out on one of the beds.

"You could sleep for a bit," my dad says, and the other bed looks so inviting after days of sleeping on the ground. After . . . Matt. But it wouldn't feel right sleeping while Noah is having a bullet dug out of his arm, and Dad and I need to talk.

We go outside, to a pair of lawn chairs beside the door, and as the sun pushes its way up from the horizon—crowding out the darkness and leaving us in the light—I tell him everything.

CHAPTER 19

CHAPTER 19

Freedom is ticking its way around the face of the old clock above the door—*so close so close so close*—when Jason Kendrick comes into the market. He gets a big dumb smile on his face as if he's seeing me for the first time. I swear to God he's a human goldfish.

"Hello there, Sparkles." He waggles his LEGO-block-man eyebrows in a way that's probably always going to make me laugh. "What are the odds of me getting out of here with an illegal six-pack of beer?"

"I guess it depends on how you feel about pretentious overpriced microbrews." Since our grocery store was dying a slow death by Winn-Dixie, Dad decided to go green. He brought in prepackaged organic foods and locally grown meat and produce. He even put a couple of bistro-style tables on the sidewalk where weekend tourists like to sit and drink fair-trade coffee. Dad claims it's business survival, but I think it's just part of the evolution of Dan Wells.

Jason, however, is not so evolved. He crinkles his nose. "If that's all you've got."

"I'll give you the family discount."

He grins, and even though he's wearing his I-am-a-responsible-adult-with-a-job polo shirt and khakis that suggest he's just come off his shift at Home Depot, there's a chip in the corner of his front tooth that I've never seen before. I'm not even going to ask. "I always knew you wanted me."

"You figured me out," I say, as he follows me over to the new beer cooler filled with brands I'd never known existed before we started stocking them. "I was only using your brother to get to you."

"Speaking of my brother, did you hear him and Gabrielle finally broke up?"

In the space that follows I check my Justin barometer for signs of life, and there's nothing more than a blip of sympathy. "I hadn't. I'm sorry."

Jason shrugs as he picks up a six-pack of maple oat ale. "Do people actually drink this shit?"

"Yep."

"Any good?"

"No idea."

"You think a girl might like it?"

"Like, a girl who's not a blow-up doll?"

Jason fake-punches me on the shoulder but his ears have turned so pink that I resist the urge to continue teasing him. "A few of us are doing a campfire tonight at O'Leno," he says. "Wanna join us?"

It's been a year since the last campfire party, but I haven't been back to the state park. It's still too fresh. My therapist says I shouldn't see what happened that weekend as taking someone's life but as saving my own. Except every single morning since that last campfire party, I wake up and have to rearrange the guilt to make room for happiness. Blame is lodged in my heart like grit in an oyster, and it feels like there's nothing in the world that can turn it into a pearl.

I don't tell Jason any of this. I just tuck the memories back into the dark, tender part of my heart and give him the most authentic smile I can manage. "I wish I could." That part is a lie and maybe he even knows it, but the next part is true. "We're leaving tonight."

"Where you headed?"

"Dad borrowed an old Airstream from a friend down in Tarpon Springs," I tell him. "We're going to spend the summer camping."

Jason's face goes thoughtful. "Ready to get back on the horse, huh?"

The therapist suggested we reclaim camping as a

family. Replace some of the bad memories with good ones. Dad and I actually talk to each other these days, and Danny's not calling himself Daniel Boone anymore. I kind of miss that. It was cute. But it's nice to have a family that's functioning again. "Yeah," I say. "I think it's going to be fun."

Dad is taking the next three months off work—leaving the shop in Rhea Chung's capable hands while we're away—so we can travel the whole United States. The plan is to start up the East Coast first. Visit Washington, DC, and New York City, and then follow I-90 across the country, stopping to see places like Mount Rushmore and Yellowstone National Park. Maybe go to Disneyland to see how different it is from Disney World. Take the southern route home so we can ride mules in the Grand Canyon and spend a day or two in New Orleans. For weeks now Danny has been packing his suitcase— Wonder Woman is ready to go—and asking at bedtime if tomorrow is the day we go camping.

Tonight is the tomorrow he's been waiting for.

"Have a good trip." Jason shoulder-bumps me. "Send me a couple of postcards and don't get knocked up."

I laugh and kiss his cheek. "I hope your girlfriend likes your fancy beer. Now get the hell out of here."

The bells on the front door jingle as he leaves, and I'm tucking my own ten-dollar bill into the register to pay for the beer when the bells go off again. "I told you to get the hell—"

It's not Jason.

The tattoos still cover his arms—stars and mermaids and sailing ships—but his hair is longer now. Dark and curling out from beneath a tan-colored ball cap so battered the fabric is peeling away from the brim. If I didn't recognize him, if I wasn't completely sure, he could easily be mistaken for . . . someone else.

But it is him. It's Noah.

Noah is here.

I haven't seen him since the Homestead police department, where FBI agents questioned us separately—the way they do on television—to see if our stories matched. Leaving Flamingo before calling the police, as it turns out, was a bad decision. It made us look suspicious, especially since Noah and I had the murder weapon, a cell phone filled with pictures of dead people, and Lindsey's phone. So I had to tell the story again and again and again, always starting with Duane dropping me off at O'Leno and always ending in a seedy motel in Homestead. Every time answering questions designed to confuse me, make me change my story.

They quizzed me on everything we did, every choice we made. And when they asked me if Noah and I had sexual intercourse, they made it sound shameful and wrong, when it was neither. I never wanted my first time to be a big deal, and now it's forever part of a federal murder investigation. Every law enforcement agency in South Florida—and my dad—knows I lost my virginity in a Cassadaga cemetery.

Finally, they let us go.

I found out later it was because Susan MacNeal—Matt's mother—told investigators that ever since Matt set the neighbor's cat on fire when he was ten, she feared he was capable of murder. She shared her suspicion that Matt had a hand in his sister's death and that she'd kept his disorder a secret because she feared for her own life. That she trusted her nephew more than she'd trusted her own son.

Two days after, a team of divers found Matt's body wedged between the roots of the mangroves—stashed for later in the crocodile's hidey-hole—near the entrance to the marina at Flamingo. The size of his hands matched the strangulation marks around Noah's neck, and the bullet wounds proved consistent with my story of self-defense.

Seeing Noah now—standing just inside the door of the shop as if he's scared to come any closer—dredges up the memories. Maybe that's why I haven't tried to contact him. And why I haven't heard from him, either. Except Noah is here. I think it might be completely messed-up to feel this way after everything that happened, but I am so damn glad to see him.

"Hey," he says in that honey-and-gravel voice of his. It still has the ability to curl my toes. He offers me a tentative grin, and it's like I have no control over my own mouth. I smile big. Hard. Happy.

"Hi."

"I, um—I wasn't sure if I should come, but—"

"I'm glad you did."

Since the first time I met him, Noah makes me want to place my truths at his doorstep, instead of keeping them to myself. I've never believed in love at first sight, but I know that feeling this way about someone is pretty rare. It might be that our shared trauma is the only thing holding us together. Maybe my imagination has spent the past year spinning him up into someone he's not. But there's always the possibility that his doorstep is exactly where my truths belong.

"Yeah?" he asks.

I nod. "Where's Molly?"

"I told her she should probably wait in the truck."

"Let her in."

He pushes the door open and gives a whistle. Molly's nails click on the wood floor as she runs into the shop. She leaps right up off the ground and licks the underside of my chin.

"You know, I've had so many things I've wanted to talk about with you over the past year," Noah says. "But I wouldn't have predicted the first thing would be the dog."

After Flamingo, Duane dropped the U-Haul pickup in Arcadia. But when he called the lady who was keeping Molly, she said Noah had already arranged to come get her. I hoped he might stop in High Springs on his way home, but he never came. My therapist suggested Noah's method of dealing might be to box up everything associated with the traumatic event and put it away. I got that. I did. But it still hurt that he never said good-bye. I push that aside to ask, "What would you have predicted?"

"I don't know." Noah closes the distance from the door to where I'm standing, but doesn't come as close as we've been. "I left Florida feeling pretty beat up. The physical aside, I was embarrassed that I didn't see Matt clearly when my own father is exactly like him. I was useless to you in Flamingo. Helpless. You saved my life, and afterward I just felt completely . . . unworthy."

"If you're going to feel embarrassed about anything, it should probably be for all the words that just came out of your mouth," I say, and the corner of his mouth hitches up in a grin. "I saved you because it never occurred to me that there was any other choice. But here's the thing . . . I would do it again if it meant keeping you in the same world as me, so spare me this unworthy crap. I care about you."

Noah reaches out and tucks a strand of hair behind my ear. It's back to blond now, my hair, and I wonder what he thinks about it. As his fingertips graze my skin, a shiver skims down my back. After all this time, he still has that effect. "It's fucked-up that I've missed you, isn't it?"

"Absolutely," I say, and he laughs in that low Noah way that's been burned into my brain since the first time I heard it. "But I've missed you, too."

We are standing so close that a breeze could barely fit between us—and I have reason to believe I'm about to kiss him—when the bells go off once more and Rhea comes into the shop for her afternoon shift. "Sorry I'm late," she says. "Traffic was crazy."

I step away from Noah, laughing, because there's hardly ever traffic in High Springs. "I'm going to have to take that fifteen cents from your next paycheck," I say, as she pulls me into a good-bye hug. "I'm sorry."

"Go home, silly girl," she says. "And have a happy summer."

"You, too."

Noah and Molly follow me out of the shop onto the sidewalk outside. "Do you have time for a walk?"

I still have to finish packing, cook dinner, and give Danny a bath, but I am officially on vacation so I guess there's no rush. "Yep." We head up Main Street toward the railroad tracks and the dueling hardware stores that sit across the street from each other. Beyond the tracks, the water tower declares this the City of High Springs. After spending so many years wanting to leave, I've finally made peace with this place. That doesn't mean I'm going to stay, but I'm okay with it being where I'm from and where I can always come home.

"How, um—you doing okay?" Noah's question is casual, but I know what he's really asking.

"I don't know." I shrug. "I have nightmares every once in a while, and I'm seeing a therapist who has to remind me weekly that I am not the monster. And I *know* that, but it's easy to forget."

Noah nods. "I understand."

"I knew you would."

"Lindsey's parents say they don't blame me," I continue. "But sometimes I catch Mrs. Buck staring at me in church on Sunday, and I wonder if she's thinking how unfair it is that her daughter is dead and I'm not. She probably is thinking that. I do all the time."

"I thought being alone might help me forget." Noah's voice goes husky for a moment, but after he clears his throat, he's back to normal. "But there's such a thing as too much solitude. Too much time to think."

"Do you still have the Cougar?"

"No," he says. "Keeping it didn't feel right."

"I'm sorry."

He shrugs a little. "It was just a car."

We walk a bit farther.

"I wrestled a long time over whether I should come," Noah says. "I wasn't sure if you'd even want to see me again, considering . . . but I regretted not saying good-bye and I figured it was probably time I said thank you."

I stop him right there in the middle of the sidewalk and kiss him. It is a kiss made of absolution and hope, sorrow and promise. And as he kisses me back, he grants me the same. His hands bury themselves in my hair, and when it ends, the back of his T-shirt is clenched tight in my fists.

"You're welcome."

"Jesus," Noah whispers into my hair, raising goose bumps on my arms and making my toes feel as if they've melted inside my boots. "Now I wish I'd come here sooner."

"Me, too."

"I was wondering," he says, as we start walking again. "Do you think we can have a do-over? Maybe slow it down. Go on an actual date and figure out if this"—Noah gestures from himself to me and back again—"is really something."

"Yes."

"When?"

"How does August look for you?"

"Too far from now."

"We're leaving tonight to spend the summer camping," I say. "We, um—my family was kind of broken when I met you. All I had was a head full of unfocused dreams and a desperate desire to escape my life. We both know how that turned out."

"Yeah."

"I have an online shop now." It feels strange to have a fond memory of Matt MacNeal, but if I have to have one, I'm glad it's this. I'm nowhere near my first million, but this fall, after Danny starts kindergarten, I will have enough money to plan my first solo trip. Maybe nothing as grand as Machu Picchu or Fiji, maybe somewhere a little closer to home.

"I've seen your website," Noah says. "It looks good."

"It feels good to be doing instead of dreaming," I say. "And this vacation—it's the first we've taken together as a family since my mom died, so I need to be with them. I want to be with them."

Noah looks disappointed, but there is an understanding in the way he nods and in the brown warmth of his eyes. "So, okay. August. I guess that will have to do."

It takes all my self-control not to tell him how—when I pulled the pins from the map on my bedroom wall—I found the pin he'd moved from New York to Montana. How I phoned several dozen state parks, trying to track him down, before I reached the one where Noah works. The guy who answered told me Noah was leading a hike and offered to take a message. Instead, I made a reservation.

Noah's fingers twine through mine, and my brain and mouth go on a rogue mission, breaking free from my resolve to keep it a surprise. "Or maybe I'll see you in three weeks at Thompson Falls."

The light comes up in his eyes as he figures it out, and when he smiles, huge and wide like a little kid on Christmas morning, I have to smile back in order to release some of the too-big-for-my-body feelings I've been carrying around. And as we walk up Main Street, wearing our hearts on our faces, I can't help thinking that maybe, finally, this is the pearl.

Maybe it's not.

Time will tell, I guess.

But, either way, it's good to have a plan.

AUTHOR'S NOTE

During a freshman literature course I did in college, we were tasked with reading short stories by American authors, including giants like Ernest Hemingway and F. Scott Fitzgerald. I loved reading the stories but was notoriously awful at interpreting the meaning behind them. (The Internet was just a baby back then, so there weren't whole websites devoted to doing that job for me.) After reading we would discuss the text in class, and I was usually surprised (and sometimes confused) by what I'd missed that the other students had caught.

One of my favorites—and one that has stuck with me all these years—was Fitzgerald's "The Ice Palace," which was originally published in 1920 in *The Saturday Evening Post*. I was charmed by how the story bookends itself (a device I've used more than once in my own professional writing life), but, more importantly, I loved that Sally Carrol Happer's struggle to find her place as a young woman in a changing world was as relevant in 1986 as it was in 1920. It's still relevant today.

The Devil You Know was heavily inspired by "The Ice Palace." Cadie and Sally Carrol have nearly a hundred years separating them, but their lives are pretty similar. Both girls want something more for themselves, get a little lost on their quests to find it, and ultimately make their way back home. Fitzgerald knew in 1920 what we know today: that it's hard to be a woman in a world filled with real and imaginary monsters.

And that there's usually more to a story than meets the eye.

ACKNOWLEDGMENTS

ACKNOWLEDGMENTS

Sometimes it's easy to forget that books don't just spring fully formed from a writer's head. Hemingway (who shared an editor with Fitzgerald, by the way) is credited with saying that "the first draft of anything is shit," and he was probably right about that. Which is why I am so grateful for Brett Wright, who pulled on the tall boots and waded in with me on this one.

My it-takes-a-village village includes the whole Bloomsbury team, Victoria Wells Arms, Kate Schafer Testerman, Suzanne Young, Cristin Bishara, Miranda Kenneally, Tara Kelly, Veronica Rossi, Kelly Jensen, Carla Black, Ginger Phillips, Anna Hutchinson, Gail Yates, the staff of Barnes & Noble #2711 in Fort Myers, and the whole B&N family, including Tracy Vidakovich, Billy McKay, and Brian Monahan. I couldn't have done it without any of you. Thank you.

Special thanks to Lee County sheriff deputy Todd Olmer and Florida Wildlife officer Guy Carpenter for the nuts and bolts of murder, jurisdiction, and the eating habits of alligators and crocodiles. Thanks for grossing me out, Todd. And I hope my portrayal of Naked Ed Watts will be seen in the light of respect and good nature that was intended.

Mom, Jack, Caroline, and Scott, I love you all.

And Phil . . . I love you best.

TRISH DOLLER is the author of *The Devil You Know*; *Where the Stars Still Shine*, an Indie Next List Pick; and *Something Like Normal*, an ABC New Voices Pick and a finalist for NPR's Best Teen Books of All Time, among many other accolades. She has been a newspaper reporter, radio personality, and bookseller. She lives with her family in Fort Myers, Florida, with a relentlessly optimistic Border collie and a pirate.

www.trishdoller.com
@TrishDoller

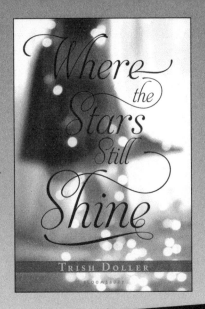

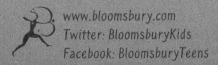